DECEMBER
in New York

The Strange Man
with the
Childish Shoes

DANIEL VALENTINO

ISBN Softcover   978-1-951469-18-4

Printed in the United States of America.

To order additional copies of this book, contact:
Bookwhip
1-855-339-3589
https://www.bookwhip.com

Contents

Prologue

The university of life is perhaps the only one in which all people, in different circumstances, and in a very particular and radical manner, learns all the necessary skills to confront life. We never formally speak of its prestige or recognize its high level of academics, but it is there that without notice, thousands of things are discovered and a lot of challenges are met. In this university, we are not rewarded or measured by grades, but the best rewards are to overcome the problems that threaten failure in relationships with our colleagues, economic distress, social problems, family, and with one's self etc. Contrary to academics, mistakes are not graded with notes.

They are paid with the weight of suffering in each one of us. In this university, we have thousands of things to discover, but way more to learn. Moreover, when humility is conquered by our own ego of feeling that we know everything, or feeling that we are superior to others, the universe acts wisely by setting guides, tutors, or teachers to show us that the greatness of things are not based on their weight, nor their size, but rather, on how significant they are. When we are capable of giving or doing something good for others, the satisfaction felt does not have a price, and even more so if we are directly responsible for drawing a smile on somebody's face.

The main teacher of this world, through his example, established that we are not only to live just to exist, but we have to live to serve, and die in the satisfaction of having accomplished with the duty of having served humanity. In this marvelous, infinite world, there exists no limit. We decide how far we want to go. We choose whether we follow an

Chapter 1

Monday, An Unexpected Encounter

On a cold morning in December, in The Babel of Iron, my mind, programmed by routine or rather, imprisoned by it, followed the tick tock of punctuality attached to my subconscious, ordered me to get on my feet. A new week has begun and there were obligations to attend to. Everything indicated that it would be a completely normal day, an ordinary day like the rest I've had before, but something in particular was about to occur. Not belonging to the brotherhood of: *witches, psychics, clairvoyants or seers,* I could not predict what was about to happen. I was simply following the orders of Her Majesty, Queen "Routine." I woke up without any deterrent, and once my sleepiness was defeated, via an intense bombarding of warm water, I was ready and willing to go out and confront a new day.

But before that, I had borrowed a few minutes from the clock, or simply put, it was my reward for always finishing everything on time in the mornings. I would deservingly take advantage of them to drink a cup of tea and watch the news on television. Well, in reality, it wasn't really the news that interested me, because it was usually the same thing: thefts, homicides, financial crisis, and in the end, it was often the same tragedies and discouraging news from every day; nothing new. I would magically

Not breaking the timeliness scheme, and looking to catch the train on time, I left my house a lot earlier than usual on that day. A fierce merciless snowstorm had whipped the city the night before. The streets and sidewalks were completely covered in dense and spongy white layer, a wonder that only nature could present us. As expected, that gift propitiated by mother nature, completely incapacitated traffic in almost the entire city, as it converted its surface into a real ice skating rink.

A little while before getting to the train station, I noticed something rather unusual. It was dominated by the rush of urgency. The emergency service, was like always efficiently making use of their privileges given to them by the transit laws, moving rapidly from one side to the other, looking to get to the place where the tragedy had occurred. A great number of people congregated near the train station waiting to get on an alternate mode of transportation. They were creating a completely different scenario than the one I was used to seeing daily. With all that chaos, it wouldn't take a genius to realize that the train service had been suspended. I would know why very shortly. What started as a normal and quiet day, suddenly turned into a day of surprises, and well, it was time to take on the challenge that come along with living in a big city where thousands of things can happen in a blink of an eye, and where being taken by surprise happens so often.

Inside the station, as I wriggled in between the people, I took my place on the platform. It was the little space that was untouchable and prohibited. The only person that could step on it was me. In fact, I could say that my footprints were imaginarily imprinted on there, thanks to my daily routine in that place's solid and impenetrable structure. I had an also been given imaginary property title, making it even more prohibited and untouchable for any other person but me. The platform of the station was full, mainly by the same usual faces; some were new because of the train delay that forced a lot of the usual and new people to coincide in the same schedule.

Among all the faces, there was one in particular that caught my attention; it was of a man standing around three to four feet from me. He had a grey suit on. I would say he looked rather normal. At one simple glance, you could tell he worked as a clerk or something along that line. What made a difference and even a good laugh, were his shoes that did not match his suit at all. It seemed like his suit was fit for going to an office while his shoes was for going to the park or to a children's party. His shoes were of a very bright color, and they looked somewhat funny and fairly childish. There were pictures of very famous comic strips on them, but I do not want to go into further details to avoid publicizing what doesn't need to be publicized. The thing is, if he was looking for attention, those famous comic strips stamped on his shoes, would create the opposite kind of attention that any look could give. Only he knew the reason why he decided to dress that way. It was not for me to know why, and it certainly did not concern me. On a daily basis, you can see some very weird things in this city, which no longer cause any wonder. You actually end up getting used to them. What he could not hide though, was the expression of sadness and concern on his face, but maybe it was normal since the people in that place looked the same, due to the train delay. There was another detail that stood out to me: on his right hand, he carefully and firmly held a notebook, or perhaps a diary, reason enough to take care of it as if it's his wife, girlfriend, or his most valuable asset. The notebook appeared to be a bit used, or better yet, I would say very old, with some of its pages loose but very well clipped to avoid losing them. After I finished my psychoanalysis, I momentarily diverted all of my attention to the rest of the people in the station. They were assuming the roles of sensationalist news reporters, dragging various versions of cause of the sudden suspension of the train service, versions that quickly began to circulate inside the entire station, becoming the breaking news of the day.

The train service had been suspended because a man had decided to end his life. He jumped into the train tracks of the previous station from where I was. No one was surprised, much less lamenting, since this is daily bread in this big city. All of a sudden, that man that I had been looking at [for the first time] approached me and with a soft and shaking voice, asked me for the time. In an attempt to bring some humor into the situation, trying and somewhat changing his sad and worried face, I said:

"Sorry my friend, I don't have a watch on, because I don't like to be governed by time."

He looked at me straight in the eye. I could see his eyes were somewhat

Obviously, it was a joke. He had been in the station almost the same amount of time as I had been there, and I had not seen anyone get close to him, or at least with the intention of robbing him. The only people standing next to him was a lady holding her baby and her purse, and myself. She seemed to be struggling with what she had. Her purse was noticeably heavy and it was impossible for that woman to have been capable of stealing from him, and in my case, stealing has never been my compulsion. That left me very intrigued because I was not exactly sure what he was trying to tell me. Days later I came to know.

We began to talk more confidently. We had to do something to kill time. We were feeling despair and impatience as we waited while the train became up and running again, so we could continue with the usual and in accordance to how routine orders it. As I was talking to this man, I felt something weird. The people around us were staring at me with bewilderment, as if they were seeing something out of the normal. You'd think that I was talking to myself, and in that case, the cause of their reaction would be justified, but I knew it wasn't like that.

Forty minutes had passed and the train was still suspended. It was clear that the repair was going to take more time than anticipated, so the only thing left to do was wait. As the conversation began to take its course, the people did not stop staring at me, and each time, it was with more and more disbelief. I really had no idea why they were staring at me with that surprised look and it truly began to bother me. I calmed down and told myself:

"Like I give a damn about what these people are thinking of me!"

I knew I was completely sane and that my senses were a hundred percent working. I simply chose to ignore them and continued our chat.

"Are you new to this neighborhood? Is this the first time you're taking the train at this station?"

I asked.

"Actually, I have lived in this neighborhood for a couple years and I always take the train in the previous station. Today, I felt a little overwhelmed and decided to take the train in this station. I wanted to take the opportunity to have a short walk, take a breath of fresh air, and try to relax and see if that will help me ease this tension," responded the man, somewhat discouraged.

It seemed very normal to me. I would the same thing on some occasions and I really didn't give it much interest.

The clock kept ticking to the rhythm of things, and the authorities kept moving from one place to another, without being able to reestablish the train service still. The long faces of concern did not cease from looking at their watches and their faces began to demand agility. Some, despite the tight space on the platform because of the great number of people, had been moving anxiously from one side to side. And what else could be done? that was the only way of counterattacking the terrible cold that hit that morning.

Other people were either reading a newspaper, a book, or on their cell phones. I imagine they were justifying the excessive delay in getting to their respective destinations. What began to become notorious were a few characters which, dominated by their despair and impotence of not being able to confront the people who were guilty of the delay, or their inability to control their rage or finding someone to take it out on, vented with profane gossips and allegations, phrases that even the most liberal of liberals would censor. I am almost sure that on that day, even the unborn were baptized by those famous phrases from various poets unleashed in fury. The attitude was anticipated since tardiness is considered a great offense even if you have a just cause. The truth is, all of the usual train passengers broke the rule of punctuality on that day. Everything was triggered by one man who decided to abandon the world of the living by dying an effective and visceral death, dismembered by a train. In the end, despite the cause, the only thing that was expected was the appropriate sanction for being late.

Going back to the conversation with the strange man with the childish shoes, he decided to ask me:

"Where is your destination?" "Where will you get off?"

"I am going to Thirty Fourth Street in Manhattan. My office is there." I answered him cavalierly.

"A very commercial area!" commented the man.

"That's right," I responded and asked him the same question. He calmly responded:

At that moment, I thought that both, this response and the misplacement of his watch, made me consider that this man was very mysterious. As I was trying to make my conclusions, I assumed he was an executive, one of those who travel from one place to another every time their bosses tell them to. In that manner, I disposed of my uneasiness at that moment. The thing is, during our entire wait, and despite of the great number of people who were there, it seemed that I was the only one in whom he could trust, or rather, it seemed as if I was the only one in that place. That started to concern me a little. For a long time, I had been riding this train at this station and never had anyone approach me and talked to me in with such ease and confidence as he did. I even dared to think that he already knew me or that we had previously been friends. At that moment, I remembered a common quote that went like: *Life is like a box of chocolates... you never know what you're gonna get...* It really was my phrase of the day because later on, I would encounter a few more surprises.

"What else can possibly happen?" I asked myself and laughed at the same time.

I had been stuck in this station for over an hour, talking to this man; enough time to know a little something about the life of someone that I had just met. And as if I was a filing cabinet, he began to store his secrets and told me some stories of what he had gone through. That hour seemed like a year, waiting for them to fix everything. I believe that time in question of obligation can become our enemy. However, I should admit that between stories after story, the wait seemed a bit entertaining.

Like any good and nosy person, I asked him about the notebook that he had in his hand.

"My life is captured in these pages."

He responded with a half baked smile. It was actually the only time I saw him smile.

"Sounds interesting!" I told him, and at the same time I asked: "Are you a writer?"

"Something like that. I am just someone who decided to write and keep my journey in this world on pages," he explained modestly.

"By the way, what is your name?" The strange man with the childish shoes asked me again.

"Nice to meet you. My name is Jeremy." I responded courteously, returning the same question.

But at that precise moment when he was about to respond to me, they announced through the speaker the reestablishment of the train service, making the stranger desist from giving me the answer I was waiting for. After almost two hours of waiting, and seeing how everything was getting back to normal, I took a deep breath and told myself: "*thank heavens it was time*". All of those long and worried faces were taking a sigh of relief just knowing that they would soon be out of that cage without bars.

Once the train reached the station and the doors opened. It was like a great marathon or competition. Everyone rushed towards the entrance trying to secure a space inside. It only took seconds before all of the wagons were full to the point of bursting, without abusing exaggeration, there was no space left, not even for air. The cluster of people gave the perfect impression of packed sardines. In this case, I would say "*human sardines packed in an enormous can*". If that machine could talk, it would have pleaded for some people to get off. Its structure could not hold any longer. It was over its capacity limit, but amid the chaos of the masses, it was difficult to act rationally, and the people only wanted to get in the train no matter what. We had waited almost two hours and I thought, five or ten minutes would not make a big difference nor make up for my delay.

"I prefer to wait a few more minutes and travel comfortably, than submit myself to the torment and indignation of being crushed by the sardines in that machine." I said decidedly while smiling at my recent companion.

"I agree, sometimes in losing you win more," responded my new friend. "That is so true." I said.

Not even five minutes had passed when the other train made its gallant entrance. Just as I had thought, this one was practically empty. In fact some of the seats were available, and I thought that it had been worth the wait, "*this trip will be comfortable!*"

I told myself, a bit excited. I thought it was the perfect reward for having been waiting so long.

was going to reign again and little by little, the heat of the train began to cover us.

Because of his accent and appearance of a traveler, I was convinced that my new friend was not from this new city. For this reason, and because I was sure of what he was going to say, I asked:

"Where are you from?"

"I'm from halfway around of the world, from a country in the Pacific coast and south of the coffee country. [Ecuador]" He responded without hesitation.

"Coincidentally, I am from the same country"

"*Brilliant!* What a coincidence!" He responded as if the coincidence had surprised him as well.

"Despite the fact that this city is the new home of people who are from the same place, it is not common to meet one of them and entail a conversation, let alone become friends," I said to him with more confidence now that I knew we were compatriots.

"It must be the fast paced rhythm of this city that prevents us from looking at our surroundings, and we only look to see what is in front of us, only thinking about what we have to do before time runs out. This routine is a constant battle that, on occasion, takes us to the edge of insanity. What better example than those people who were trying to get onto that first train. They didn't care about trampling over one another. The only thing that mattered to them was getting on. It is as if we are programmable machines, and like a spreading virus, we all end up infected by the eagerness of everyday life and the fast paced rhythm of others," commented the man very lucidly.

"That is very true. I am one of those people myself." I told him jokingly.

I had just finished pronouncing the last word, and again, I could feel the bewildered stares of all the other passengers, piercing me like daggers. Everyone was looking at me as if they were scared or shocked, and there were others who looked at me with pity and shame. I became very uncomfortable and began to sweat. In fact, a woman sitting to my left looked at me and turned her head. As if murmuring words of accusations, she got up and moved to the edge of the seat in front of us. She was very uneasy and every so often, she would look back. It was as if she felt threatened and was avoiding getting close to me. In any case, she did not want to be close to me. It was then that I secretly began to look at my clothes. I began with my shoes because I thought that perhaps I had stepped on something that was causing foul odor. I saw reaffirmed that they were clean and nothing was on them, so I moved to my pants. I looked for stain or imperfection, but again I saw nothing wrong. Finally, I looked at my coat, but it was in vain. There was nothing strange there either, so I found no reason to deserve such accusations and I became more worried. My brain began to burn some of my neurons as I formulated questions trying to find a damn answer to these accusingly baffled stares. Something serious must be happening. It was not by mere chance that in the station and inside the train itself, people were acting this way toward me. I knew I was fine. My mind, my feelings, and even my heart rate were all coordinated to perfection, but considering that manner of staring at me, my subconscious made me doubt for a couple seconds. I was a little agitated and scared thinking in euphoria:

"Damn it, I am not crazy! Nothing on me is so strange that these people would have reason to stare at me this way."

Everything was pointing to the fact that the only person who could hear and see that man was me. All of these people were looking at me as I talk to someone who did not exist, and that was reason enough for them to think I was crazy. It was the closest answer to the ironic logic of the thousands of questions that filled my head. Despite that, getting to that conclusion took me to a state of uncontrollable panic, but at the same time, I tried to stay calm, staying with the idea that this was impossible. In fact, I had always been a sane guy. The only thing I wanted to do at that moment was to get to my stop, get off the train, forget this ever happened, get to work, and for a moment, deal with my boss regarding the extreme delay and let the rest of the day go on as usual.

Conflictingly, at that moment, all I wanted was my frustrating routine. I then decided to calm down a bit, but there were still a few stops left to get to my destination. There was nothing left for me to do but to ignore everyone and continue with my journey. From that moment on, I tried to he was the cause as to why these people would think I was a lunatic. So then in a soft voice I told him:

"Have you noticed that people are starring at us in a very strange manner, as if we are some scary strangers, especially me?"

Very calmly and serenely, he said:

"That is how it is. In this city, remember that we are foreigners and they don't want a lot of us here. It must be that. Try to stay calm and take this advice: no matter what I do, I never pay attention to the rest of the people unless that they really need it or they inspire confidence, because a lot of people only dedicate themselves to criticizing and judging others without any justified reason only with the desire to accuse."

He had an answer to everything. He took everything very calmly, and nothing bothered or worried him. It seemed that he just simply wanted to live for that day and that was it. Seeing there was no other way out, I decided to follow his advice, which for a moment seemed to be working. Anyhow, the whole situation did bother me. During some instances, doubt would cloud my reason. It was a constant battle in my head, between the various questions and the lack of answers. Amidst my reveries, I was able to hear the announcement of the stop on Forty Ninth Street through the loud speaker. I had been anxiously waiting for that moment.

"Two stops! Only two more stops and this will be over!" I told myself, taking a small sigh of relief.

When the train doors opened, I saw the woman, who had made me feel like a freak when she moved from her seat, walk out, perhaps because I repulsed her or scared her. Three more onlookers walked out with her. At that moment, I took a deep breath that filled me with life again. There were only two or three people left on the train, but I ignored them completely. In the meantime, I waited for the freedom that I was bound to feel when my stop arrived. Those twenty minutes on the train were the torture I had never suffered. They felt like an eternity compared to the two hours that I had been trapped in the station.

But during that time when the train was about to close its doors, a man appeared out of nowhere and held the doors from closing. It was as if he was the owner of time. Very tranquil and with much exaggerated patience, he began to load a bunch of junk onto the train. The odor that filled the clean air in the train, his tattered clothes, and his totally unkempt appearance, clearly pointed to him being an outsider a wanderer, a vagabond, or a "hobo" as they call them here. Slowly and with ease, he began to bring in all his things one by one.

"Again, another darn delay!" I thought with ire.

But I could not complain, because the privilege to board a public service like this one, was all his. There were a lot of boxes and bags that began to fill various seats. Finally, he brought in a shopping cart that was full of weird objects and recyclables. Once inside the wagon with a mess that took up quite some space, the train began to move. The few onlookers that were left on the train dashed out due to the foul smell. Courteously and amicably, he greeted me. I responded very respectfully and he also greeted my friend, who also responded to his acknowledgement. At that moment, I wanted to stand up and jump with excitement. I wanted to scream to the faces of all those skeptics who did not stop staring at me and thought I was a lunatic, demonstrating to them that I was not the only one who could see and speak to this man. But it was all in vain, for the only ones left on the train were the three of us. I lost the momentum and I said to myself *"what the hell!"* I didn't have to prove anything and much less, prove to anyone my mental state. It was enough that I knew that I was not the only one who could see my companion, and that was sufficient proof that I was fine.

The distance between one stop to the next, considering the speed of the train, was short. Four minutes had not even passed and my stop was coming right up. But before the doors opened, I told my new and strange friend:

"Well this is my stop. It was a pleasure to meet you, and have a good day."

I extended my hand out, waiting to see him to do the same as good manners would dictate.

But it was not so. He instead grabbed my shoulder and said:

"Pleasure was mine, thank you for your company. The best of luck today, and I hope to see you soon!"

He left me with my arm extended. It did not worry me because all I

"Have a good day and may heaven bless you."

"Thank you, same to you," answered the stranger, with a spontaneous smile.

Getting off the train had never been so pleasing, and with all freedom, I directed myself to my place of work. When I arrived, it was normal my boss to be waiting for a good explanation, and I was expecting the luck of not being the only one affected, but unfortunately, it wasn't so. I told him what happened and surprisingly, he smiled and said:

"Don't let this happen again, eh!"

But his comment was not enough for me. I wanted him to understand and

I said:

"For this situation not to repeat itself does not solely depend on me." He seemed not too worried about it, and responded:

"Ok young man, go to your place. There is work that is behind, you will see."

I took my tools and went to my spot, but not before saying hello to the rest of my colleagues. I began doing my duties to justify my salary, but I struggled to concentrate. The memory of what had just happened would not let my mind rest. That Monday flew by in a blink of an eye. The clock read five in the evening, and it was time to leave. The ride back home was very peaceful, and the people were not accusing me with their stares, despite the fact that I was having a conversation with a girl from work. I was just trying not to remember what had happened, but it was impossible. What I wanted the most was just to get home, take a hot shower, and in my privacy, try to calmly analyze everything that had transpired. That day was one of those days which I would not prefer to remember for anything in this world and I would like it better to just archive it in the hard drive of obliviousness.

When I got off the train, I took my usual route back home, but not before I made a necessary stop in the store close to the train station, to buy a lottery ticket. Christmas was around the corner and the jackpot prize was huge. If luck was on my side and would smile at me with at least a little part of that jackpot, I would stop being a slave to the queen of routine and liberate myself from her. That situation would make me think of taking a long vacation. Hassan, the owner of the store, ceased from being my friend, because he occasionally would recommend some numbers for me to play but would always remind me that if I won, I had to share the winnings with him.

"Old man, that is a given," I would say to him. We always joked around. The snow that fell the following morning had been almost completely removed and a great part of it, without a doubt had returned to its natural state, which helped me walk faster, escaping the cold and freezing air that comes with this time of the year.

It was as if there was a Congress meeting or a reunion of old lady gossipers. My roommates were sitting around doing nothing. They were just hanging out laughing at each other's laughs, which were unmistakable and loud. You could hear them as you entered the house. Once I opened the door and went inside the apartment, they began to interrogate me about what had happened.

"I'm not a hundred percent sure. I only know that someone jumped onto the tracks, and it caused the train service to be suspended for a while. I got to work late and the people would not stop staring at me as if I was a lunatic. Today, which seemed to be a good kick off for the week and was supposed to be completely normal, turned out to be fatal, what else can I tell you."

I commented something confusing about what had happened.

Danny, one of my friends from the apartment, making mention of what happened, put on the news for me, specifically on what happened that morning. The news of the day was about a man who had been dragged by the train and that one of the wheels had severed his arm, completely cutting it off from his body but he was still alive due to the quick intervention of the emergency medical technicians who assisted him and took him to the hospital. He is in critical condition, with a not so encouraging prognosis. Sadly, I thought about this man and his sad story. I hoped he would recover soon.

"It could happen to anyone. Life is in constant danger, the only thing we can do is entrust our lives to the Lord so he can always protect us." I concluded, and proceeded to do my household labor.

that the hot shower that I wanted to have. I stayed in there a little longer than usual. I was so tired because of everything that had happened. After I ate dinner and prepared a few things for the following day, I went to bed. But not even five seconds had passed and my mind began to work as if it were a Ferris wheel. Each event that happened that day began to play over and over again in my mind, altering my neurons once again and thus began what would be a long and sleepless night.

The hours went by. I could only hear the deafening tick tock sound of the clock, and because the silence was so overwhelming in the room, it sounded like a hammer banging against the wall. I could not find a way to get to sleep. I was tired of counting sheep and whatever other animal passing through my head. I got up disoriented and a bit upset, and I made my way to the kitchen to find something that would help with this insomnia. At that moment, I remembered a magic tea that my grandmother would give me when I was a child. It never works, but I always made her believe differently because I wanted her to feel good. I would not lose anything by trying it. What if, with a little luck, that tea would help? As I crossed the living room, I went near the window and I could discern that the night was very peaceful and apparently calm, save for what seemed to be light rain hitting the glass with a synchronized rhythm. At that moment, the clock read fifteen minutes after one in the morning.

In that precise moment when I began to prepare my grandmother's magic tea, something flashed in my head as if it were an emergency. I left what I was doing, went back to my bedroom, turned on the computer and began writing: step by step, detail after detail, everything that had happened that morning, from the moment I woke up and opened my eyes, until the moment I said goodbye to my new and mysterious friend. I was thinking somehow that this would not only be an interesting story but also a very real one. Of course, every now and then I would add and exaggerate a little more to make it more dramatic, just like how the editors do it in the tabloids.

Each of the events that had happened that morning led to the conversation that I kept with that mysterious gentleman, and thus began my encounter with this stranger. It was an encounter that would begin to occupy space in the hard drive of my computer, and justify my first night of sleeplessness.

At that moment, I forgot about everything. All I wanted was just to write and write. My eyes were nailed to the screen of the computer and my hands to the keyboard, working together as a team, not wanting to forget any part of the conversation I had with this man at the train station: a man that for a short moment of time, would pass and become a part of the list of my friends. The two hours I spent being trapped in the train station unleashed such an intense talk with this stranger that crossed my path in a very mysterious way. It was a talk that, without realizing it, was touching on social and political issues, making a reference to this last one, was the reason this stranger had to undertake a long and difficult crossing for daring to do something that was worth of admiration.

With respect to politics, I had to confess that I was not an expert nor had knowledge of the subject, but I was aware of a few things, at least with respect to that of my country, and that helped me maintain the conversation, or at least, flowing with that interesting issue.

It all started with a question that the stranger asked me, which is what elicited such an intense conversation. Fortunately, we agreed in almost in everything. To the contrary, I could imagine that we would have been the characters of another tragedy.

"Why are you in this country [USA]," the stranger asked me.

That question seemed a bit strange to me. No one had ever asked me that before… well, except the Immigration officer who stamped my passport, giving me permission to enter this country, and of course, the answer [I gave him] was totally different from the one I gave back then.

"For the same reason why a lot of us are here or trying to get here… as they say, this is the land of opportunities. Well, I came to find mine." I answered very frankly.

As if it was an interrogation, he asked me again:

"Do you believe that there are no opportunities in our country?"

"Opportunities are everywhere. It is up to us to know where to look for them and to take advantage of them, but unfortunately, they are very for which they were elected and thus forcing people like you and I to have to flee from our land." I answered, a bit indignantly.

"Regrettably, this world moves by a system in which we all have to follow. There is nothing wrong with that, what is bad is the main artery, which is politics. It is made up of various cancerous cells that end up contaminating the rest, and I believe that politics is the mother of all evil, and harlots are the key and the perfect sanctuary to commit crimes and misdeeds in the frameworks of legality. Look at what always happens: a corrupt politician steals millions, squandering it on nonsense, but because he is immune by his same condition, he is seldom prosecuted. A poor devil submerged in misery, thanks to such system, steals a bread to eat to survive a few more days, is condemned to a few years in jail, while the true guilty criminal who is part of such system, is free to roam and no one can do or say anything. Justice is only for the weak. A lunatic without brains but with power can feel like the he owns this world and he can become very dangerous," commented the gentlemen, a bit upset.

Those words seemed a bit harsh to me but I totally agreed with him. Taking a breath, he continued with the following:

"To give you an example: would it be fair if one day I would go and interrupt the peace in your home where you are with your family, and making use of my power, I'd accuse you of being a suspect of something that I don't even know about. I go into your house and I, looking around, found something very valuable to you, which could be the fountain of your income and the livelihood for your family, yet it is also important to me, and it would help in making me very rich and powerful and I need to have it. I begin to devise a scheme that will somehow make you look like a delinquent and someone who represents danger to others. Abusing my power, I would make you disappear from your family and I'd take what I want. If there were to be protests, I wouldn't care because I have accomplished my objective, knowing that what I did was dirty and illegal, but just as how the saying goes: *here governs the law of the jungle.*"

For me, that example was clear and easy to understand. I knew exactly what those words were referring to and I kept the thread of the conversation by saying:

"None of us would like it if someone comes into our home in that manner, and even worse, if they take away what is ours. Power is very permeable. It could easily be affected by ambition and hypocrisy, but above all, by the money that could probably buy the conscience of the most honest person. Take a look at Judas, for a few coins, he sold out his master. What can we expect of others? I even include myself in that list because I am not perfect; and just like everyone else, I could succumb to any temptation at any time."

"Yes, this is true. Having power requires a great amount of responsibility and if this person would use it correctly, for good, everyone would truly benefit from it. But on the other hand, it represents danger, and the victims are always the most innocent," commented the man.

"Unfortunately, it is the truth," I answered, validating his words.

By his expression, it seemed he was trying to vent. That morning was the precise moment for it and he found in me the perfect receptor and listener. To tell the truth, I am not one of those people who like to pay attention to anyone, much less, have such an extended conversation; if I did, it was because of the train delay and because I had to do something to distract my mind to avoid losing it. Besides, the conversation seemed very interesting because without a doubt, we were on the same wavelength, which facilitated the dialogue.

I filled myself with patience, the mother of all virtues, and knowing that the train service was going to take some time to get fixed, I was again willing to listen to my friend.

"Do you think telling the truth is bad?" The man asked me again.

"Well, I don't think telling the truth is bad, but it does have its consequences depending on what or who it involves."

I responded vaguely.

With the patience and peace of someone who has no qualms, with fervent passion, and as if he was liberating something he had inside, the strange man with the childish shoes began to say:

"In our country, to tell you the truth, and not to agree with those dealing with power, it is considered a crime, and you can even be categorized as a traitor, conspirator, and rebel.

We were tired of so much corruption, excessive embezzlement of all their disgusting, dirty, and fat behinds on a chair without sweating one drop, and obligating the rest to go through risky undertakings just to survive.

We were tired of seeing a group of swindlers, each one with two or three assistants and these too with their assistants, in their barn that was named "Congress," to make it more elegant. They would make a huge feast with the treasury getting fatter and even more their bank accounts and wallets by selling their dirty consciences. I think that those swindlers, if they could just sell their mothers or souls, would do it for sure since they would do more to feed their greed than work for the people. Their hours of work were marked with insolence and even then, they created overtime. Their hardest work was done by warming up a chair for some hours. As if that was not enough; they kept receiving bonuses and economic benefits that they themselves created using their disgusting wiles: "what the law gives them." Why in the world then do they not apply the exact same law for the all workers in the entire country?"

That gentleman was questioning himself, while anger began to draw upon his face.

After a small pause, he continued with his story saying:

"Basic rights like education and health fell apart. Hospitals with long lines of people who were condemned to die because their fundamental right was denied, children wagering their lives adorning the streets trying to make a buck to buy food, a father and a mother working long hours to make some miserable dollars to try to get through the day, with the uncertainty of what tomorrow will bring.

Tired of all the filth, my friends and I decided to arm ourselves with valor, to go out and protest and reclaim the rights that were being violated. There was no other way out, and seeing that this was the only way to mend the error that we had made by electing such dishonorable people, there was nothing else to do but consume that purpose although it wouldn't make a difference because of the damn corruption and the dirty politics that contaminated our society. They [politicians] were like hundreds of insects waiting in line for the moment of truth in which they could take over those positions available. It is like saying that when a bad one left, ten worse would come in, making the cure worse than the disease. Government was steadily declining. There were no good politicians but rather "the lesser evil." Trusting them, since there was no other option, we ended up electing them and they end up becoming the same history and the same story that never ends."

"None of these would have happened, and we would not have been a joke or a laughing stock if our leaders were more honest and would dedicate themselves to governing in a correct and loyal manner, based on the fact that the only thing our society wants is its well being and progress a right which, to this day, has been totally denied. Among the politicians are: the bad, the worse, good for nothings, the clowns, and the puppets who are nothing more than shoe shiners waiting for the best offer from the group mentioned." I responded somewhat worked up as I listened to a part of his story.

"It is a shame that our small country is dominated by sewer rats which only contaminate and infect illnesses to an honest person," my new friend concluded.

At times, the tone of the conversation was rising. Well, it was to be expected. We were talking about true political gems that continue to be outright disgusting …nothing more and nothing less.

Deeper into the issue, after I listened to part of the story my new friend had just narrated, I became repulsed, discontent, and angered by the gut of those damn swindlers, so much so that I could not resist giving my own opinion:

"We are stereotyped as corrupt in the eyes of the world, thanks to such brilliant characters. The outside world think that we are all like them [our politicians], and that is not even true. People that are honest, just, and above all, hard working far outnumber a group of dirty consciences, those that have exemplified that negative image throughout this entire time. Our country needs a profound detoxification to eliminate all of that garbage of politics which, for years, has put a ransom on our future, our well being, and our rights, flushing our image down the toilet."

"You are right, but unfortunately, that is a truth that we shouldn't ignore," said my new and strange friend, putting a cap to the conversation that morning.

characters], they wouldn't exactly be phrases of love; there would not be enough time to do so, bile would invade my entire body, and even my computer's hard drive would be full to the maximum. Well, maybe I am exaggerating a bit, but it is to express that behind the curtains of politics, there is an entire repertoire of stories that need to come to light. It is not worth spoiling the moment. Even those slags do not deserve me staying up so late to talk about them. That was what I told myself in the precise moment that I was going to turn off the computer and lay down to try and get some sleep.

From the moment I went to prepare my grandmothers celebrated tea until I turned off my computer, three and a half hours had passed. Time was not on my side again, and with the freedom given to mark the rhythm of things, a huge part of my sleeping time had been taken. Prisoner of an overdose of tiredness and sleeplessness, I ran to my bed, but prior to that, I made sure that this was not going to get me the next morning. Wanting to be in sync with routine, I set the alarm of an old wall clock to six thirty in the morning. That's the time I usually wake up every day. I would set this alarm only in extreme situations and in case I suspected that my sleep would be as heavy as lead. Surely enough, that early morning was one of them. I could have sworn that not even ten minutes had passed when I closed my eyes and that blessed alarm began to go off with a loud noise, reminding me, in the most abrupt way, that I should get up and begin my everyday struggle.

Chapter 2

Tuesday,
A Premeditated Encounter

It was Tuesday, and another day of labor to accomplish. Despite the fact that my weariness called me to bed, I did not let myself be tempted because those types of weaknesses in this city have an expensive price tag. After taking a shower that brought me back to life, along with my cup of tea, I sat and watched the news, waiting for the weather report to see that beautiful blond character again, the owner of those exclusive minutes reserved only for her. That woman had become my most beautiful obsession. I would never get tired of looking at her. She was beautiful like the cherry trees that bloomed in the spring, and of course, it was obvious that behind that loveliness were a whole lot of admirers, that like me, would content themselves with seeing her through that window of magical worlds. I know very well that there are things very far from our reach, but thanks to dreaming, they do not cost anything. Perhaps we can't have them, but at least it helps bring them a little closer, even if it's just for a few seconds. I am not ashamed to admit it because for me, dreaming was the only way of detaching myself from the disenchantment to which the mundane confined me to, every day. Those minutes spent watching the beautiful blonde woman became my biggest and inaccessible dream, my

That day, my platonic love advised that bursts of ice cold air from the north was strongly whipping through the city, making the temperature even more frigid. Taking into consideration all of her warnings and following her advice, I left exaggeratedly prepared and willing to battle even the coldest temperatures after saying goodbye to her. I had just gotten over a terrible cold a few days before, precisely for not following the advice of my favorite TV personality. Sometimes we think we are superheroes and believe we are immune to everything, thus my foolishness took me to suffer a chronic cold that incapacitated me for several days. But it had to happen to teach me a lesson: to be more responsible and above all, be more careful. This time, I was not going to let the same thing happen to me, so I took my warmest hooded coat, put on a cashmere scarf over my neck and mouth, and I left.

After saying hello to a few neighbors, which coincidentally have the same schedule as me every morning, I went to take the transportation which, day after day, would do me the favor of taking me to my place of work. Despite the low temperature, the walk to the train station was very tranquil. The trifling amount of snow left on the streets and sidewalks had totally been removed, which made walking a lot easier. On my way to the train station, my head, as if it were a motor of meditation and memories, began to again remember everything that had happened the day before, thinking suggestively if I was the only person these things happen to, or on the contrary, there might be others with me on the same boat, so to speak.

I found myself beginning to experience a sensation of feelings. On one hand, I wanted to forget the schizophrenic episode that had occurred on the train, and on the other, I felt a desperate urge to find this man again and know the rest of the story that he had begun to narrate. *It wouldn't be right to stay in the middle of the story, or that I would have to invent an ending myself.* That is what I told myself as I walked toward the station. That is why deep inside me, even if it would implicate almost peeking into the threshold of madness, I wanted to meet my friend once again, whether he was imaginary or real. Most of all, what I wanted was to have something to write about, and that could be a once in a lifetime opportunity. *Oh but what the hell, whatever happen happens.* I ended up saying as I was willing to confront whatever was to happen.

When I arrived at the station, I noticed a relative sense of calmness and everything seemed very peaceful. I took a deep breath and said: *Thank heavens! It seems that this day is going to be normal.* For doing my good deed for the day, I missed the 7:10 train. As fast as I ran, I wasn't able to reach it on time. I arrived only to see it off. The two minutes it took me to help a lady carry her baby and her stroller to the train station was responsible for missing the train. I did not worry about it because it was for a good cause, and anyhow, the service was running on time, so the next train would arrive shortly. As I got closer to my usual waiting area by the station, my eyes gave notice to the presence of my new friend, proving that wishes do come true. A few minutes before, something deep inside me wanted to see that man again, and the universe, playing the role of an infinite genius, granted my wish. In fact, my new and strange friend was standing on the same place I found him the day before, but there was a certain curiosity that I needed to address. *Why didn't he get on the train that just left?* Clearly, you could tell that he had been at the station longer than I, and he could have easily boarded that previous train, however, he didn't. *Could it be that he also wished to see me again, and for that reason decided to keep waiting?* Whatever his motive was, it didn't matter at that moment. *What new surprises would life have for me today?* I thought with somewhat of a nervous smile as I began to approach him. When I stood in front of my friend, I stopped and looked at him with a friendly smile, indicating my greeting. Since I forgot to wear my gloves, my hands were inside my coat pocket to warm, and I did not want to take them out and expose them to cold air, if at all possible, even if it may seem to be discourteous to him.

He had a peculiar way of dressing. You could say I am a good observer. It was impossible not to look at his odd wardrobe that incidentally made me unsure whether it was the same [or another of the same] from what he had worn the previous day when I met him. It was something which, for a moment, caught my attention, but then I remembered that various people in this city usually have the same style of suit and even the same color, to somewhat simplify their time of dressing, trying to avoid an argument with their personal stylist. Despite his clothes being peculiar and striking, it did not seem to bother him one bit. As the cold made the rest of us look like vegetables in a freezer, it didn't seem to bother him at all. I needed to consider this detail because it was simply impossible to ignore. But well, despite his strange form of dressing and attitude toward this frigid weather, contrary from the day before, he seemed very calm that morning.

"Hello, good morning! What a pleasure to see you again! I see you came to this station to take the train. What made you decide that?"

After saying hello to him, it was the first thing that occurred to me to ask. "Despite the cold, the walk I took yesterday made me feel good; so good in fact that I decided to spend a few more mornings for walking, hence I came to this station to take the train," He responded.

"You should do the same." He added, putting a smile to his words.

"In fact, I walk a lot but I normally do it in the summer when the temperature is fit for it. Frankly, I am scared of the cold."

I answered smiling, with the purpose of extending our conversation.

Upon remembering that the day before, he mentioned something about contacting his superiors, I wanted to know how it went with them, so I asked him:

"Were you able to contact your superior yesterday?"

"Yes, in fact he decided to leave me here for a couple more days to finish something I needed to finish, and only 'till then will the Superior Advisor decide on the plans he has for me."

He responded in somewhat of a mysterious way.

I really did not understand what he was trying to tell me with those ambiguous words. *What Supreme Advisor was he referring to? What was it exactly that he did?* I didn't know, but well, I kept listening to him to see if these questions could be cleared up. I continued:

"Everything seems to be so peaceful and calm today, such a contrast from yesterday, which was truly a chaos."

"Yes, let's hope that the day will end with the same tranquility and calmness it started with, because none of us would want to pass through the same crossing we went through yesterday."

I answered even more calmly to continue the conversation.

"There are things that are inevitable and unpredictable. They occur in a blink of an eye. We do not own time or the future, not even our own lives. We are here just passing by, receiving orders from superiors, and as such, we ought follow them and meet them with calmness, but above all, with a lot of patience. I can see that you are very patient and calm."

He said assuredly.

"With situations like the one that happened yesterday, there is not much one can do to change its course. If it does not depend on us, then it is far from us to try and avoid them. The option I always take is to wait for things to get back to normal or for things to just simply calm down. The terrible situations that I had gone through throughout my life have helped me learn to be patient and most of all, take things calmly. Besides, I do not want to age before my time, making my life bitter over nothing. The only thing that it would accomplish is to have the years become more noticeable on my face, filling it with wrinkles."

I said with a joking laugh, and he ended up laughing too.

The train service was running on schedule. There were not a lot of people in the station and the few people who were there were at a considerable distance from us. That is why I felt comfortable talking to him. I did not have all of those accusing stares all over me which that made me feel like some weird oddity, like a being from another dimension, or worse, like I was a lunatic. Today, everything was very relaxed, and I was not going to let anything or anyone mess this moment up.

After a few greetings, a few questions, and some laughs, the train arrived to the station and… *bingo!* This one was quite empty and it had some seats available which contributed even more to the tranquility of that day. I am not sure if it was because of custom or because I was one of the thousands infected by the routine. I went to board the train the same way I did every day, entering through the same door, getting into the same wagon, and sitting in the same seat. It didn't seem strange that my friend did the same thing and sat next to me. It only took a few words into our conversation when a couple sitting in front of us began to murmur and stare oddly at us, making me feel uncomfortable and pissed at the same time. Trying to avoid ruining the moment and messing up my day, I applied the same advice that I gave myself: promising that nothing or no one will ruin my day. I decided to ignore the entire world and forget about

Between stops, people would get on and off, and I was gradually getting close to my destination. I am not certain if it was destined or otherwise, or if it was simply a coincidence, but that outsider that I encountered the day before was again adorning us with his presence, doing exactly the same thing he did. He got on the same train, precisely the one we were on, but this time around, he got on one stop previous to the one the day before. *Life with its things in a maze of surprise, which surprises us with something new every day.* I thought in that moment.

When we got to Fifty Seventh Street, the train barely opened the doors so people could get off. The outsider came in with his shopping cart filled with his things, in between the doors, and stopping the doors from closing as he dragged the rest of his things. His odor was so strong that it was understandable why people were leaving terrorized, trying not to get their clean and perfumed clothes contaminated by the smell, or simply because they could not stand the odor. That scene made me laugh and gave me the satisfaction of laughing back at them.

I was only a few stops until my destination. I did not care and I remained in that wagon. It meant I had to endure the unpleasant odor of our new companion. But that odor was compensated by his amicable gestures and the happy person beneath all of those rags. I asked myself at that moment the circumstances which may have led him to live in that condition, but I preferred not to make inaccurate hypothesis, and judge him falsely.

His basic deficiencies, including living arrangements and food were compensated by a great charisma and an exaggeratedly amicable and happy personality that despite not having enough [or almost nothing] to survive, except for his own will and great faith towards the unseen, one could clearly tell he was very happy. In fact, he was a lot happier than all of those who, despite having everything, continue to complain, showing great unconformity towards life, creating a big pit in their lives which, by no means, is filled by any material possession. Perhaps not by everything, but I even include myself on that list, because on some occasions, I too have complained about life, but thanks to the example of this man, I learned to value [and be grateful for] what I am, and what I have.

When the outsider finished bringing all his things in, he sat in the seat in front of us with the smile that characterized him. After saying hello to my friend, he extended his hand to greet me and said:

"Hello! What a coincidence, and what a pleasure to see you again! I can see you don't have the worried expression you had on yesterday."

"Hello! Well yes, it is a big coincidence indeed! The terrible chaos and the mishaps I went through yesterday, add that to my tardiness in coming to work, is what made me show that face, covered with the mask of concern. You know how the rules are in this country. Rules are rules, and we have to respect them."

I said to him as he reached his hand out, and I returned his greeting. "Thankful that I learned to live with time and making it my accomplice, I stopped being a slave to those rules that hold many as prisoners of their own freedom. Perhaps I may have nothing to eat and no place to sleep comfortably, but I have the most special and marvelous gift life, two legs to walk through it, eyes that let me admire its incredible beauty, and a heart that inspires me to be thankful for what I am and for what I have, every morning as I wake up."

He said with a peaceful expression, adding or rather advising me that if I happen to go through a similar situation, I should remember those last words: wise words that only a person with a lot of experience, reflected on the grayness of his hair, was capable of expressing.

"Advice very well taken. Thank you so much." I said, thanking him for is words.

"Mathew, where are you going today?" My friend asked the outsider.

That is how I came to know the name of my other new friend. Well, I already considered him that way, although I might not ever see him again.

"I am going to Brooklyn to look for my daily portion of meals. And just as there are many who marginalize us by thinking that we are a problem or a plague, there are also others who have concern for their fellow men and share what little they have."

Responded Mathew.

"You think I can go with you?" My friend asked him. "Of course, there is always room for one more." Mathew answered him.

"And afterwards, what will you do?" My friend asked him again.

"Having no prior commitment for today, and not having to report to

Nothing seemed to worry or bother him, as if it was his task to fully complete. He was simply there to live, day after day, being happy.

"You know what Mathew; it is not a bad idea! Besides, it is a good option to stay away from this terrible cold outside. If it wasn't for the time or the fact that my stay here has been shortened, along with some things that I still have to do and to finish before my superior tells me where my new location will be, it would be a pleasure to accompany you and take a stroll in one of your mobile homes; but I will take a rain check for another occasion. Oh, and I will pay for the coffee, okay?"

In a joking manner, and laughing, my friend answered to Mathew.

"There are much more important things to do than taking a nap or going for a stroll, especially when it is about accomplishing orders given by superiors. Go in peace, do what is important first. I know that you will be free and will be able to have all the time for yourself very soon. You are going to be able to go anywhere without having to show any passport or personal identification, because everything that your eyes will see, all of it, will be yours, and when you come back, please do not only bring coffee, include a donut, or better yet, make it two because coffee without the donuts is just not coffee."

Mathew answered my friend, as he laughed. "By the way, what is your name?"

Mathew asked me after that laugh.

"My name is Jeremy, my pleasure. I apologize for not introducing myself." I said to Mathew, with some regret.

"Well Jeremy, you too are invited to the breakfast but please, when you buy the coffee, do not forget to include an extra order of donuts. I am somewhat of a glutton and it would also be nice if there were leftovers to eat for the next day."

Responded Mathew as he gave me a big smile.

With that suggestion, he ended up giving me an invitation for which I did not know the place nor the date, but I had a pending invitation to have breakfast.

"Yes of course! It would be my pleasure to bring you your request." I answered, thankful for the invitation.

It was just laughter after laughter. Whoever saw us must have thought we were crazy. In fact, the expression of anguish and sadness in which I had upon meeting my friend had completely disappeared. Seeing Mathew's happiness, as well as mine, had spread to him as well.

Amid the laughter and somewhat strange conversations between Mathew and my friend, which I did not understand, the train was getting closer to my destination, just on time, and punctual as always. As Mathew reminded me not to forget the invitation for breakfast, he said goodbye to me, stretching his hand out, and my friend did the same.

"Thank you! May heaven fill you with blessings! Now, don't expose yourselves too much to the cold!"

I told them as I walked off the train.

That scene was a copy from the day before. I got off at that stop to go to work while they stayed on the train… but to where? I didn't know but I had to find out.

This time, as I got to work, I was punctual as usual and a few minutes before I started, I took the opportunity to sit at the dining room table next to all my co workers to share breakfast, talk, and laugh with them for a while. And as in every good conversation between men, the most important thing could not be left out: the most beautiful and best inspiration… women were the main topic of our conversation, almost every morning. It was a healthy way to kill boredom and we needed inspiration to begin our day well, waiting for the clock to strike five in the afternoon so we could go home.

That day, despite it being tiring, went by smoothly, without any delays. Once I caught up with all my work that lagged behind, I set out for home. The clock struck five o'clock in the afternoon, announcing that it was time to leave. My workplace was located almost in the downtown area, while my house was only minutes from crossing Fifty Ninth Street. The distance between Manhattan and Queens was relatively short. It would not even take twenty minutes from the time I get on the train to reach Thirtieth Avenue in Astoria, Queens, the station where the train would pick me up every morning to go to work and drop me off every evening to go back home.

Upon leaving the station, I stopped by my friend, Hassan's store as I

I was taken aback upon catching a glimpse of the emergency services assisting some persons who, minutes before had been victims of a terrible accident three blocks from the train station. There had been a collision involving three vehicles, caused by irresponsibility and over speeding which was prohibited in residential zones. As I approached the scene, I saw the paramedics giving first aid to two of the victims. One of them was a young woman. Some meters from that scene were firefighters cutting the twisted metal to free someone trapped inside of their car. It had been hit hard by the other vehicles involved in the accident. Taking into consideration the old adage that goes <<*curiosity killed the cat>>* I was already very safe and sound at home, before anything like this could happen.

After doing all of my chores and getting things ready for the next day, as I usually do, I remembered that I had enough material to pull up an all nighter again, I sat in front of my computer and I continued with the story that I had begun to write the night before.

The silence in my room, my computer, and the old wall clock that marked ten o'clock at that time were not only my witnesses but also my accomplices in having another sleepless night. My hands, serving as the USB connection between my computer and my head, opened the file that had not yet been named, much less, given a title. The only thing I marked it with was a personal note to identify it. The important thing was that it contained my first hours of insomnia which told this story, and it was gradually taking form. Agreeing and being totally convinced by those who say that everything one does is the best, I let myself dream for a couple seconds, as I joked with myself saying: *"If I could make this get to the theaters, I would surely be a millionaire",* I began to laugh, but did not snap out from dreaming.

After fixing a few spelling errors and discarding all the fictitious details, thinking that it would no longer be real, letter by letter, word by word, I began to transfer all the information that was in my head. Well, whatever corresponded to the conversation that I had with my new friend anyways. All of this information had to be put into the hard drive of my computer. This was the one place where it would be safe.

"What results came about from the protests?"

Starting from the last line as I left it a night before, it was the question that helped me regain memory of the conversation I had with my friend that Tuesday morning.

With a very lengthy answer, and somewhat subdued in tone by the anger and the impotency reflected in his eyes by not being able to do anything to change the course of history, my new friend continued his story saying: "Because of the contaminated politics that practically controlled our entire country, our efforts and intents to somewhat clean that garbage were rendered just the way it was nothing more than intentions! With the majority of our colleagues in prison and us being entrenched under walls and a roof, our future seems totally uncertain. For our sin of coming out and demanding our rights, we were condemned to live in secrecy, being persecuted like fugitives, while the real criminals are still left in power stealing, committing crimes, and doing their using mischiefs without anyone saying or doing anything about it, turning the country into a major negotiated politics."

Unable to hold back my curiosity in know the rest of the story, I asked: "What did you do then? Knowing that the authorities were on to you?" With anger reflected on his face as he remembered everything he had gone through, and taking his time, he responded:

"To avoid the police from bursting into my home for the information they had obtained, through punches and tortures, from three of my colleagues who were arrested days earlier, I decided to flee and spare my loved ones from any harm. As I fled, I realized that this was something I should start getting used to.

Packing in a small suitcase all the love and the image of my family, especially my daughter as my most treasured memory, along with some clothes for the one way trip, and accompanied by friends, I was ready to embark on a journey without knowing absolutely nothing of what was going to happen ahead. Only trusting and laying my well being and future in the hands of the unseen and heavenly, I left with the hug of my daughter, mother, and sister in the memory of the unforgettable. It meant a flood of great proportions and an earthquake of intensity one thousand on the Richter scale that tormented all I had within me.

It was a Sunday, a little before midnight; after traveling secretly for a long and uncomfortable fifteen hours, I found myself sitting a few meters thing I needed to cross the border into the neighboring northern country. That country was my second home for a long time and from which I only have marvelous memories.

The universe, being the infinite genius that it was, granted my wish of traveling the world. It was a wish I had since childhood. Of course, not the way I expected it, but he knew what he was doing. Besides, I still had several pending wishes and I was not going to claim them or run the risk of not having them granted. The one thousand and one adventures, the madness, and the occasional mischief that I lived through with my friends remained packed as great memories during the moment of my departure. With a great tempest in my eyes and with the hope of one day exchanging boredom for an overdose of adrenaline rush, I marched out leaving behind on the other side of the border everything I had lived through with my friends, and especially my family. The only thing I took with me was the reality of knowing that true friendship does indeed exist; and that it wasn't something which only happens in the movies. These exoduses, like a stealing dog, took me to perforate the invisible but very well marked border of the neighboring northern country. It was ironically the price a corrupt system gave me in exchange for my freedom."

My new friend could barely hide the sadness behind his story. His face and expressions was in sync with what he was explaining. Even then, he continued to narrate his story:

"Once inside the coffee country's territory, I came to the City of Eternal Spring [Medellin] after a prolonged two days trip. Imagining being in a luxurious hotel room, I borrowed a seat from one of the bus terminals to spend the night on, in full view of the local passengers who would not stop looking at me. They, without a doubt, would wonder <<*where did that stranger come from?* >> The stay in that "luxurious hotel room" turned out to be very uncomfortable. I drifted in and out in my sleep and woke up with sore muscles. I felt more tired than I was when I laid down.

That morning, I let a coin toss decide where to head to next; and with the answer at hand, I left the terminal and saw a totally different sunrise from what I was used to. I was ready and willing to find an adequate place to stay until I returned to my route up North, which was my actual objective.

I was walking around the city somewhat lost, wandering aimlessly. I just let my instincts take over. I came upon a small park and stopped there for a break under the refreshing shade of one of the trees. After a nice and heartwarming time of resting, I heard several applauses that seemed to have come from a crowd a few meters away. I got up and followed the steps of my curiosity. Like a good stowaway that I was, I squirmed in between the people to see who deserved such ovation. The artist was nothing more and nothing less than a little ten years old boy and his little eight years old brother. They were dressed as clowns, juggling, singing children's songs with a humorous touch. They were improvising a small circus that did not charge any entrance fee. They were just letting the people put a price on their talent and that is how they made a living every day.

Delighted with what these two little boys were doing, I sat down to see their show. It was then when I realized that I was the only one left with the two little superstars who were taking a short recess while preparing for the big six o'clock show. This was the most important time of the day for them basing from the amount of people that would pass through the park on their way home. It was that show time which the meal for the night would depend on, along with the breakfast the following morning, for the two young superstars and their family back in the house.

The little superstars, greeted me in the most unconventional [street smart to be exact] way. They were very respectful and well mannered. One of them greeted me, saying:

"My name is Lucas. I am ten years old and I am the clown called *"Crazy Lucas"*."

The eldest of the little superstars introduced himself to me and presented his younger brother William in the same manner, whose superstar name was *"Laughter"* because of his original and unique way of making people laugh.

After giving me their welcome, they shared a small piece of bread that was leftover from lunch and named me as their guest of honor for their spectacular evening show. I did not want to be discourteous to such generosity, kindness, and hospitality, so I accepted their invitation but under the condition that I would pay for their dinner that evening. With their faces etched with happiness and savoring what they were going to and I didn't even care where I was going to spend the night in. That very special moment was priceless, and I just had to take advantage of it.

The universe, through the law of compensation was giving me a gift: a little of that love that it had abruptly stripped from my arms the love of my precious daughter and my family. I was convinced that the universe placed these little ones along my path, so that with their show and happy disposition, all my sadness and worries would be sent straight down to hell.

The little superstars opened the spectacular show of the evening [just like they had announced it] with a song interpretation performed by Laughter, while Crazy Lucas took the role of the master of ceremonies. As they performed, they asked me to watch over their belongings, and since I was no longer a regular spectator, they had me seated next to the improvised stage, on an old bench in the VIP section. They offered me all of the amenities to enjoy the show in the best possible way, so I really felt like a special guest. With several deserving applauses given for to their stellar performance, the little superstars dropped the curtains that evening with the satisfaction of having accomplished their task successfully. It was evident by the good amount of money they collected. Each of their performances: the different acrobatics, juggling, and songs deserved that applause, not to mention their funny jokes conducted at my cost, but that didn't bother me at all. Laughter is the medicine for the soul, and thanks to them, my soul was very happy that evening. Once again, the universe showing me a big lesson on courage and survival, placed these two little teachers along my path so I could learn from their example.

During our most awaited dinnertime, Lucas could no longer hold back his curiosity and asked me:

"Where are you from and what do you do?"

Trying to be very accurate and not to entangle him with all the details, I simply told him that I was a neighbor, visiting his city for a short period of time. Expecting Lucas to continue with his interrogation, I mentally prepared to respond in a simple yet clear manner, but it wasn't necessary. Lucas abandoned the conversation at my simple response. I think I underestimated him, and on the contrary, he understood that we should not talk about this subject further.

After the enjoyable and entertaining chat, the delicious meal, the great company, trying to escape the darkness of the night, and explaining to the boys that I had to go and look for somewhere to stay, I thanked them for all of their kindness and bid them farewell. All of a sudden, my heart began to race when William held my arm and asked me to watch over them, and in exchange for the protection, they would give me a place in their home to spend the night. After a few minutes and an incessant plea from Lucas, I was impeded from leaving. I don't know why they were so afraid to go back home alone if they were so used to it, but the sensitivity in my heart and conscience, without a doubt, made me give in. Whatever city, no matter how peaceful and safe, the darkness of the night often carries danger especially for two little boys. They could easily become prey to the danger that does not discriminate age, gender, and much less, does not understand compassion.

Things don't just transpire just because. Everything that happens to us, every event in our lives, commonly known as destiny, are numerically ordained and coordinated to perfection, waiting for the day and the hour in which the universe decides to make us play a role in it. If life had decided to put those little ones and me on the same path, it was because we mutually needed each other. It was not because of some simple coincidence. Nothing ever happens by chance or coincidence. Everything that happens is duly predestined to in a certain way, and that is how it has to be. It was for this reason that I did not resist.

With happiness on our faces because of the great company, Lucas and William asked me to buy an extra plate of food for Cenelia, their "*Fairy Godmother.*" It's what they call her. We were surely not going to starve, or well, at least not for that night. We left the restaurant laughing and telling jokes as we headed to their house. Half way to their place, William began to feel very tired and after a long day of work, he fell asleep in my arms. Lucas, on the other hand, was very active and served as my tour guide without ceasing to laugh.

After traveling for almost an hour by bus, we arrived to their home. It was located in a very poor area, along the extreme East side of the city. It was a small house with two rooms divided by several pieces of cardboard, with an improvised kitchen right by the entrance. Despite being very door opened, inside stood their *"Fairy Godmother"* Cenelia, very worried and concerned for they had taken too long to return. She was a woman in her sixties or seventies and had a chronic illness in her bones that made her depend on a walker to remain standing. Lucas presented her to me, and she was very grateful to me for bringing the children home. She invited me in to take a seat in an old yet comfortable sofa next to the kitchen, a few steps from the main entrance. That couch became my bedroom for a very long time. Lucas reminded me that this was my home and asked for a goodnight kiss and a blessing from Cenelia. He then marched to his bedroom to sleep, taking with him his little brother William by the arm.

Those extraordinary situations made me ponder that life gives us the most awe-inspiring gifts after such great sacrifices. I am sure that if I had not gone through that situation of being uprooted, I never would have known love in the midst of humanity. Now I am sure that right under our noses, there are things, places, and above all, amazing people which ideological borders prevent us from seeing through a veil of prejudice.

Cenelia was grateful for the food we brought her. She shared a little of it with Charlie. She sat next to me to talk as she enjoyed her dinner. She obviously had to ask me where I came from and how I arrived in their city. Hence Cenelia and I began a long conversation that would open a new door in my life, because every person you meet is a new world. She, who struggled to walk and was bereaved, ended up having such a huge heart and she offered me her humble ranch to stay in. I felt that her words contained happiness and sincerity when she offered me her home, and seeing how well I had gotten along with the kids and now with her, I did not see any inconvenience in staying in their house. I thanked them immensely for their generosity and promised them that I would help with the household. She jokingly mentioned that an extra helping hand was always welcome.

After a while and after listening to me with all the trust in the world, as if she had known me all her life, [I even dare compare that trust with a mother towards her child or a sister towards her brother] Cenelia opened her heart to me. She took me on a trip down her memory lane and trying to avoid falling into and drowning in her mental blackouts, she gave me a brief anecdote on how the children came into her life. It was inevitable for her to go into moments of nostalgia, followed by a stream of tears that streamed her memories and her face.

In those painful memories, Cenelia recounted one Sunday afternoon when she met two little boys crying desperately, looking for their mother who had been missing for a few days. They knocked on her door. Lucas was just five years old and his younger brother, William, was three. Cenelia wanted to make their tears stop rolling down their eyes, so she invited them to her house. Wisely taking the opportunity of their innocence at such a young age, knowing that they would believe anything she tells them, she convinced them that their mother had gone to another city to work to buy them the bicycles that they had always dreamed of, and that she would take care of them for a few days until their mother returned. Cenelia did it with the purpose of waiting for their mom to return and look for them. But five years had passed since that day and the boys still continued asking for their mother, sitting every morning by the entrance of the house with the hope of seeing her arrive with their bikes. With the patience, love, and kindness that only a person with such a big heart like Cenelia's, she was able to heal and replace the profound sadness of those two little angels that came into her house and into her life and freed her from her loneliness. The universe, reminding her that, *"parents are those that raise a child, not just conceive them,"* through a tragedy, Lucas and William sent compensating for the children she was never able to have.

With big tears in her eyes streaming straight from her heart, Cenelia told me the real reason the boys were without their mother: the naivety and immaturity of a young neighborhood girl, who blindly fell in love with all of the words and empty promises of several cowards that after using her and leaving their seed in her womb, fled like rats being preyed upon by their hunters. Stupid men who boast about the many women they have had in their sentimental lives, without realizing that a real man is not one who has many women and lies and abandons them. A real man has only one woman. He respects her, takes care of her, values her and knows how to make her happy. A real man does not run to his friends and boasts about his adventures. He stays and confronts and assumes all

She decided to leave, taking her four older children with her, who were really not a big burden [to her], and abandoned the two youngest, leaving them frail and defenseless, abandoned to luck, waiting for a miracle to watch over them and take care of them."

Showing remorse for what he said, the strange man with the childish shoes made the following comment:

"When selfishness invades us, we hurt others or those we love without realizing it. We don't consider that sooner or later, it will come back to us with interest, from the Supreme Judge who is just and fair. This summary of my life made me remember that there is something new to learn every day. It made everything that I discovered, every wonderful person that I met, and every story that I heard and lived through. It became my true school."

After taking a long, deep breath that helped dissipate the sorrow, he continued with his story in the following manner:

"Giving me a goodnight hug, Cenelia walked to her room, but not before offering me a blanket to cover myself from the cold that the morning would bring. That old sofa became my makeshift bed. I also unjustly interrupted Charlie's sleep. He had been sleeping there for a good while but I made him come down from what was going to be my bed, saying, *Sorry my little friend, but you have to look for your own space.* I lay down and after just a few minutes, Charlie paid me back in kind, with his howling and barks of despair that interrupted my sleep and reminded me that the intruder was me.

Seeing that there was room enough for the both of us, and avoiding a big battle over nothing and not being able to tolerate his howls and barks of lament, I let him sleep by my side but with the condition that he keep his fleas away from me. Charlie's warmth, combined with my terrible tiredness, made my mind and body relax, and I entered into a deep and deserving rest.

The next morning, the delicious aroma of coffee that filled the whole house and the caresses of Charlie's tongue on my face, thanking me for giving him space on his own couch, made me wake up from the deep and comforting sleep that I had fallen into. Lucas and William, having suspended their artistic activities, had taken the day off to attend to their guest.

Taking a break from their usual custom of sitting in the front of the house and waiting for their mother, they stayed inside that day and played by my side anxiously waiting for me to wake up, so that they could invite me to a very special place they wanted me to see. It was a place where they would go to, but only on special occasions.

Cenelia, charismatic and hospitable as always, asked me if Charlie's howls and fleas let me sleep. She gave me a great morning by inviting me to taste the delicious coffee she had just prepared. My mind, taking a leap into time, drew a picture of a very familiar scene like this, taking me to a magical *déjà vu*. It was a very special gift to start the day in the company of incredible and wonderful people, surely, not with the amenities that they had, but with the kindness of a family. Nonetheless, it was completely unknown to them but they made me feel at home and at the same time, richly blessed.

With the responsibility of any adult, Lucas and William despite being so young, showed a great maturity like any other old finance expert, they had given Cenelia almost everything they had collected from their talent show the night before, just keeping a minimum amount to buy their much deserved candies and for their personal savings accounts, which had just one purpose and objective very well defined.

Abusing her trust and taking advantage of the fact that I was in the land that produces the best coffee, I could not resist asking Cenelia to fill my cup for the third time. Besides being a lovely person, a good mother, a sweet, tender and very accommodating *"fairy godmother,"* she was also an excellent cook. Reason enough for Lucas and William to be very happy with her, and let's not even talk about Charlie the number one spoiled brat in the house. Without being an expert on coffee, I dare affirm in total assurance, that never in my life had I tasted such delicious coffee as the one prepared in that house.

Making her feel like the queen of the house with three subjects serving and pampering her, once we finished that delicious and nutritious breakfast, we began cleaning up the table, washing the dishes, and cleaning the rest of the house. Charlie rejected the idea of being one of the subjects helping with the chores. Despite Charlie's vagrancy, we finished our house chores right on schedule, as the kids had planned.

Asking me to keep an old a notebook, where they had all of their finances written down, with every accounting detail, and asking permission to go out, they asked for a kiss and a blessing from their guardian. Just like what they had promised, Lucas and William took me to that special place they talked about so much that morning. It was more than a special place, it was a secret place. Only the two of them knew about it, well, Charlie too, but he did not go that day. Since he did not help with the household chores, he was left at home as his punishment and was not given permission to go on the trip.

My two little friends took me to that very special place. As if they were great treasure hunters, they kept a lookout in a very mysterious and careful manner, making sure that no one was watching or following them. It was approximately twenty minutes away from their house. At a glance, there seemed to be nothing special about it. It was a small forest that struggled for survival in a tract of vacant and forgotten land which nature had condemned to be a no man's land. In fact, despite its morbid vegetation, it would still give a breeze of fresh and pure air. But I would soon find out why this place, which did not seem any different, was so important.

Lucas asked me to do him a favor of keeping a look out along with his brother William. He went towards Mickey, an old oak tree which the kids had baptized in honor of their favorite character, which coincidentally was mine too. Mickey had become the most unconditional and permanent watchman and a faithful and silent witness of the treasure that these kids had kept under its shade. Lucas then removed a thick layer of scrub that had been intentionally placed there to cover the prints and expunge any evidence that would reveal the site of the treasure. He proceeded to dig and take out from underneath the soil a small wooden box covered in several plastic bags, which had been wisely wrapped around it to avoid the moisture of the soil from damaging the structure of the box. They asked me to help them do the math by counting the money inside. Making sure again and again that the amount coincided with the accounting written in the notebook, they proceeded to put the money in their small weekly deposit box, very happy to have added a few decimals to their fortune. They again proceeded to close and cover it with the plastic bag, just exactly how they had left it the last time. Lucas joked with Mickey, asking him to guard and triple their fortune. The box went into its place, covered with a big layer of scrub, exactly how we had found it.

Surprised and at the same time moved by what I had just seen, and not being able to hold back my curiosity, I asked them:

"Why or for what purpose do you keep that money there?" Taken by his innocence and naivety, William responded: "We are saving to buy our bikes".

But Lucas, being more assertive and demonstrative that he was the man of the house, and having a very clear objective on how that money was going to be spent, responded:

"It's been several years since our mother left for another city to work so she can buy us our bicycles. I'm sure these bikes must be very expensive thus making it difficult for her to save enough money and buy them; hence she is obliged to stay apart from us longer. That is why my little brother and I decided to save this money: to go and look for her and to tell her that we no longer want the bikes. We want her to come back to us along with the rest of our siblings who we also miss very much".

That response tore my heart into a thousand pieces, causing me to have an abysmal reaction between what I wanted to say and what not to, leaving me short for words. The unconditional love for their mother was much stronger, so great that they had forgotten the pain she had caused them when she abandoned them. The lie which Cenelia invented stimulated with each passing day their innocent hope of seeing their mother again. From my young teachers, I not only learned about survival, friendship, and brotherhood, but I also learned about love, and the most amazing thing, forgiveness. With a deep breath, I buried the secret I knew about their mother, giving them the hope of seeing her again one day.

Lucas and William were satisfied with the result of the mission and thought it had all been successful. Assuring themselves that this was enough reason to celebrate, they invited me for a walk through the city. Taking the opportunity of being in one of the warmest and most beautiful cities in the world, with two amazing guides by my side, and thinking take the bus to the northern border, complying with my travel itinerary for the next day.

Before we began our journey, we had to make a mandatory stop in their favorite candy shop to buy the reward for their effort. Because of their kindness and invitation of touring me around the city, along with an unrestrained craving for the delicious delicacies there, the payment for tasting the sweets was on me. I wanted to keep up with Lucas' and

William's age and decided to put aside my grown up mask in exchange for my kid mask, which by the way, I hadn't used in years. I sat at the table with them for a long time, eating and drinking all the wonderful and delicious treats within sight, making our bodies produce an extra amount of insulin to regulate the level of sugar running through our blood. That sugar overdose was justified and well deserved.

We made sure we had a good portion for Cenelia and one for Charlie too; and not having any more space in our stomachs for more, Lucas jokingly commented that the three of us would make the best clowns. He then painted my face with chocolate in front of several customers and employees of the candy shop in that paradise. They could not stop laughing.

After many laughs and a sugar rush, we were ready to begin our tour of the city. Allowing myself to be taken by the curiosity of my two little guides, we went where they wanted to go. After visiting several beautiful and very interesting touristic places, appreciating the colonial and modern architecture that, together, made a beautiful and one of a kind contrast, enjoying the charm and the beauty of its people, [especially the women that gave that city its extra magical touch], we ended up at an makeshift exposition and sale of bicycles. It was located in a little green space, blocks away from the bus terminal the place where we had to make our last stop before heading back home. The faces of excitement and at the same time, sadness in Lucas' [especially William's] face kept me from going to the terminal to get the information I was looking for. Their afflicted expressions made me postpone my trip for several days, making an unexpected change in all my plans, forcing me to reprogram them.

William asked me if I had ever had a bike with the excitement of knowing what it feels like to ride one, since he was just conformed to looking at it from afar. That gift, as if they did not deserve to have it, had been eluding them for a very long time. Applying the lessons of goodness, gratitude, friendship, the value of giving and receiving [that they themselves had taught me in such a short amount of time,] and well, saving some phony Santa Clause's work, I used a part of my traveling budget and made that gift finally arrive into their hands, immediately eliminating their sadness.

To the designs of the universe, nothing is said. We are mere instruments of good or bad behavior which, at the enjoyment of the privilege of free will, makes us who we are. We decide what rhythm to dance to. All of the plans that I had previously intended were interrupted by the universe which made me reprogram, reminding me anew that it is not what we want that gets done, but rather, we ought to follow the pattern of events and successes assigned to us from the moment we were born up to the moment we die. Without a doubt, this was another test life had put in front of me.

Lucas and William thanked me with a strong hug from each. They made me take the driver's seat as we used the bike as transportation to get back home. It was, in itself, an adventure. Despite the fact that I was just somewhat of an experienced pilot in riding bikes, I assumed great responsibility for I was in charge of the safety of my two little teachers and tour guides. Filled more by emotion and the desire to drive than to get home early, Lucas and William switched roles from being teachers to being students, asking me to teach them how to ride. I helped them maintain equilibrium to avoid falling off. Making sure that traffic was completely clear, I let them ride on several sections one at a time. What would normally take us an hour to get home by bus took us around two and a half hours. It was the two and a half hours filled with nothing but laughter, two and a half hours that took me back to my childhood, making me decide to keep my kid mask on for a bit longer.

Despite the punishment of not letting him out, Charlie was the first one to receive and happily greet us, as always. Grateful for having kept Cenelia company and taking care of her, he deserved an extra portion of the delicious delicacies we brought for them. Cenelia, in comparison to the night before, received us very calmly. Even if we arrived very late,

Lucas and William were very happy and excited, and getting completely ahead of the explanation I was about to give, came in with their present. Cenelia was very surprised and happy at the same time. She asked them how this had come about, and before she could say another word, I hugged them and interjected:

"This is so you will never forget me when I'm gone."

The joke that Lucas made while at the candy shop came true. In the middle of the exquisite meal that Cenelia had prepared with all her care, I asked if I could be a clown and if they would let me work with them. Lucas jokingly emphasized that I did not need a costume since I already had it on. Squeezing my hand, he welcomed me into their prestigious guild of comedians.

After practicing several tricks, juggles, songs, preparing the scene for the next day and indicating my role for the show, the children thanked me with a strong hug for having helped in making one of their dreams come true. They then went to bed, reminding me that I had to be awake and cheerful for what awaited us. Cenelia did the same, letting me continue practicing my act.

Obliging Charlie to be my audience, I began rehearsing everything my two little teachers taught me, thinking how I did not want to let them down during the show. Charlie became bored of my dismal performance and he fell into a deep sleep. Not having anyone else watch my act, I laid down to sleep, waiting to get over this long and exhausting day.

Once again, the delightful coffee aroma, Charlie licking my face, and the bustle of the kids who had changed the practice of waiting for their mother into falling off their bikes several times, awakened me. After the delicious breakfast that Cenelia had prepared and leaving Charlie under her care, we left for the place where our improvised show would take place. I was going to my first day of work while they were going to continuing with their daily routine that had been interrupted by my arrival to their home. As we came closer to the place, anxiety and jitters began to take a hold of me. It was my first time doing something like this, and I could not turn back because the completion of my fare money depended on it.

Doing away with the anxiety and my nerves with some courage, I was ready to start the part of my show. I was only waiting for my little teachers to give me an order to begin my acting career. *With the errors and blunders that every beginner makes"* that were rapidly minimized by the great experience of my team, I had successfully achieved the challenge of becoming an actor. To have been my first time acting, I didn't do it so bad; well that's what I thought. Despite my many errors, we were able to make a decent payment for our talent, in fact making more money than in any other show, but it still was not enough even if the guild had a new member and the profits were not reflecting that much. Working in that rhythm it was going to take me at least two months to complete the money for my trip.

A little after dinner, while trying to find a way out of my problem and taking advantage of the fact that I know how to play guitar, I proposed to my two young colleagues to add a little live music to our show, with the purpose of innovating and attracting more people. They very happily agreed, but there was a slight problem we did not have a guitar, and I did not want to make my pocket's deficit any bigger. Cenelia suddenly stood up, went to her room, and came back with a box in her hands. Solving the problem, she opened the box and gave me a guitar which she had stored for years. It was one of her dearest remembrance of her husband who had parted to his eternal rest. Despite of it being very old, it looked new because of the good care she had given it. It only needed a few tuning and it would be ready. The sound that it produced was entrancing and lovely.

Without a doubt, its maker was a true genius. Before going to bed, we decided to practice several songs which they used to sing, and added a few new songs to their repertoire which included a small choreography that they themselves conceived. Once we readied our new strategy to bring in more curious people, or rather, more audience to our theatre, and with Cenelia's applauses that forecasted our success, we went to sleep.

Once again, concern came over me, turning my sweet hours of sleep into long hours of blasted wakefulness that ended up completely triumphant. My subconscious took advantage of my insomnia, yelling out to me to write down what it wanted to say. I took a pencil and paper and began jotting down everything it dictated. Adding melody to the words using the guitar, I was able to create a song based on a real story. It turned the main characters were Lucas and William. At that moment, the anxiety of presenting it in our theatre and exposing what I had just created began to consume me, making my insomnia a lot worse. Risking getting booted off the guild, [especially by Lucas, who was the leader and the decision maker] I decided to remain quiet about the song, letting it be a surprise at the end of the day.

My sleeplessness not only made me compose a song, but it also brought out my culinary skills. Exchanging the delicious coffee for an old blender which made a loud noise every time I stir up one of my favorite smoothies, which I decided to accompany with crispy tortillas and scrambled eggs [my expertise since it was also easy to prepare,] I made everyone awake much earlier than usual. It created a completely different atmosphere upon the start of the day, an atmosphere different from what they were used to.

After tasting a simple breakfast made with a lot of love, cleaning the whole house right after, and receiving a big ole good luck hug from Cenelia, we found ourselves in our make shift theatre, getting ready to begin the first show of the day. On that occasion, Charlie was allowed to accompany us as his reward for showing exemplary conduct towards Cenelia, and besides, it was part of his weekly days off dedicated for walking and having fun. We decided to paint and dress him up as a clown so he could help us earn his food. As we had foreseen, the live music we incorporated into our show, along with the well wishes from Cenelia, began to cause a positive impact, helping to cap our first show with great success. It was a good sign of what the rest of the day would be like. At the same time, it gave me the assurance and the confidence of not making the same mistakes which I debuted a day before.

As the day went by, we were able to close each of the show marvelously. We only anticipated the stellar performance that was going to be our *acid test*. After the break which we took advantage of to rest for a bit, drink some refreshments, and play with Charlie, it was unbeknown to us that we were already at the start of our spectacular performance. A good amount of audience gradually flocked, enticed by the music and the voice of my two young teachers that lifted everyone's spirits, filling all the seats of our improvised theatre. We broke the record of the number of audience that day, creating the perfect ambience I needed to show off the product of my insomnia turned into a song. A few minutes before closing the show, amidst the sound of applauses, I asked Lucas and William to sit by my side as I began to sing. The next two minutes would tell the story of their lives… and it said:

On his painted face, a rude reality was drawn.
He exchanged his school and books for work, there was no time to play.
He had mouths to feed, even if his costume reflected happiness,
In his heart lived a dark solitude.
Juggling and swirling with his life,
He earned his food from the streets.
The harsh life made him fend for himself,
and his childhood dreams left behind.
His home was an old carton box, with a window that he himself made.
And every night, he would look towards the heavens, looking for his mother.
Looking at a star, he asked God where his mother is,
and why she was taken to a place unknown.
It was that day when his mother abandoned him.

The applauses and cheers that I expected to receive after finishing the song were crushed by a deafening and terrifying silence which lasted for almost a minute. It was a minute when the entire audience looked at me, including Lucas and William. It felt like an eternity, leaving me confused and completely immobile, desperately waiting for some kind of a reaction from anyone. Then, Lucas gave me a hug and it turned the silence into a state of panic for me. With a round of cheers, applauses, and yells for an encore, which sounded like deliverance to my ears, we ended our performance.

Our *acid test* was an overwhelming success, reflected by the considerable amount of money we collected. Because of that, I was able to complete the money I needed for my fare and even with some extra for going out and celebrating. It was something incredible. Unable to contain our happiness, after packing all our belongings, we took Charlie, placed him between the three of us, and made a group hug at the end of the show. Our *"fairy* positive audience feedback, and for her patience and kindness towards us. We took her to a restaurant it wasn't the most luxurious one perhaps, but it was the most friendly and serene in the city, and they prepared the most exquisite food.

Without ever imagining it, I came to be a part of the lives of a very special family that taught me that one doesn't need money to be happy; that one can get by with having little, or even nothing. You just have to arm yourself with faith, and above all, charity in knowing how to share what you have. The amount does not matter, because after all, the universe compensates twice as much to those with a kind heart.

While we ate, Lucas kept telling me how much he loved the song. He asked me to talk about it and explain the inspiration behind it. Trying to be very careful of how I would respond so as not to dampen his hope of seeing his mother again, I simply told him that the song was from an artist in my country, and that I thought it seemed very timely to sing it during our final performance. With that, whatever doubt forming in his head was cleared. Cenelia became confused because she did not know what we were talking about. She asked us to explain the missing bits and pieces. Lucas helped by William, who incredibly memorized almost the entire lyrics, sang it as part of the explanation she asked for. Moved by the message and overcame by her sensitivity, she couldn't hold back her tears as she looked at me. The only two who knew the message and dedication of the song were Cenelia and I. It was a secret we kept very dearly.

Taking advantage of that special moment and the fact that we were all gathered together, I deigned to thank them for their hospitality, kindness, trust, and most of all, their friendship. I reminded them that I was only going to be with them for two more days. At that moment, the children's faces were assailed by sadness. Despite the short amount of time I spent with them, a special bond of friendship had developed. It was actually more than friendship, I would say, it was more like brotherhood since I considered them more as little brothers. And as for Cenelia, needless to mention, she was an extremely special person with a great charisma to match. She gave me well wishes for my trip and reminded me that her house was also mine. She also told me that their doors were always open for me, awaiting my return. She will always be very extraordinary to me. I will always have her in my heart."

My friend, the strange man with the childish shoes, ended his story that day with sadness reflected on his eyes, leaving me with the curiosity of anticipating the rest of the story he was narrating.

"It must be interesting to know new places, but above all, new people."

I said, after listening to his story that was getting more and more interesting every time.

"Making that trip was the best decision I have ever made in my life. I am grateful to have come to know marvelous places and amazing people, but also, discovered the true meaning of life. If I would have the opportunity to make the same trip again, I would in a heartbeat," responded my new and mysterious friend, with sincerity mirrored in his eyes, filled with the emotion his story caused.

The mysterious appearance of my new friend and the experiences he went through not only produced the best story I've been waiting to write, but also turned into my school for some reason. Apart from demonstrating great valor and unwavering fighting spirit, each of his life experiences, as told in his story, validated his sensitivity and his humanity that made me reflect, giving me a different perspective of life. So much so that I wished morning would come so that I could put into practice what I learned from a couple of sleepless nights.

The story I began to write made me lose notion of the time, taking me to the most critical point of my sleeplessness and the most addictive state of curiosity in knowing the rest of that story which became more and more interesting every time. The only thing I wanted at that moment was for morning to arrive so that I could meet my strange friend again and continue feeding my curiosity. But for the darkness of the night to be dissipated by the light of a new day, I would have to wait for two more hours.

Believing that my sleeplessness and weariness were going to sedate me, and pleading to my old wall clock's alarm not to fail me, I programmed it to go off at six thirty in the morning as always, as I took advantage of those two hours before I began my day dreaming of my girlfriend. I was certain that when we meet, she was going to hold me accountable of how

But alas, not even the dreams I had of her, nor the wakefulness, nor the exhaustion that took a hold of me, were able to sedate me. My curiosity began to fall into the most chronic point of addiction towards what I was writing, making me completely forget about everything, and taking me to a parallel world inhabited only by my computer, the continuation of the story, and the stranger and I. Never in my life had I been as interested in something as much. I had always been a cynical guy. Perhaps it was for that reason that the universe put that strange man along my path so that his story could make me see that the world was not only the four corners of my walls, but on the contrary, there are fascinating worlds to discover, each with wonders and greatness spiraling all around me and I didn't even take notice because I was only looking at one direction. Whatever the reason was, the first step was already taken. I only had to wait and see what was to come.

Sparing my old wall clock's alarm from the work, and observing the first rays of light that sneaked through my window blinds like professional burglars, I got on my feet minutes before the alarm went off, canceling the tasked I assigned it accomplish, avoiding the loud noise from filling the entire room. My new day started that way... it was Wednesday.

Chapter 3

Wednesday, Two Steps Beyond the Limits

The fatigue and insomnia I had over me had to flee and find another victim, due to the comforting warm shower I basked myself in. Changing the doses of tea for a greater dose of caffeine to help me stay awake, I sat to look at the news on television, I mean, to see my platonic love as I normally do every day before leaving.

My girlfriend, though she was very liberal, would certainly become jealous of the woman who owns my attention every morning. Although by seeing her, I wasn't doing anything to merit condemnation; I was simply admiring the perfect beauty of creation, loveliness that the universe, baptizing its perfect masterpiece on a woman, gifted this world the best daily inspiration. But to avoid misunderstandings with my beautiful girlfriend, the secret of my platonic love was very well kept between my television and I.

Receiving the last advices of my amicable love, I left to take the train. The cold temperature that visited us the day before had left, and though it still left a hint of cold, but the temperature was a lot nicer than the day before. The streets and sidewalks were totally clean, complemented by an amazing sense of stillness. It was something that was not common in this

The story that was stored in the hard drive of my computer entered into an intermediate point where turning back or cancelling the work was not an option. The only end was reaching my satisfaction. I'm not sure whether the universe granted my petition or if it simply acted on its own accord but the man with the childish shoes was again standing at the same place where I had found him. *It seems that my story will have an ending after all!*

I told myself, as I approached to greeted him.

"Hello, how are you? What a coincidence to see you again!" I said, as I went near him.

"It is not a coincidence! In case you don't remember, I told you I was going to take the train at this station this whole week."

He responded smiling.

"You're right, I forgot about that!" I said with a spontaneous smile. "How did it go yesterday?" I asked him again.

"It went marvelously well! Life is so beautiful that you only need to come close to the window and see the light of day, and it's enough to be happy."

Dissimilar to the prior two days in which he seemed sad and worried, he was much happier that morning, so much so that he was able to contaminate me with his joy, convincing me to do something I had never done throughout my entire history of taking a train at this station.

I began greeting everyone passing by me. A lot of them were surprised, but returned my greeting very courteously; and others simply looked at me as if I was nuts and chose to completely ignore me and just continued with their own business.

"I see you're learning how to look around you."

He commented, a bit surprised but satisfied with my new attitude. Somewhat surprised by his comment, I asked:

"How's that?"

"I bet you a thousand to one that throughout the entire time you have been taking the train at this station, you never said hello to some of these people, who are generally always the same ones, and they never do the same to you. But if you had done what you just did from the onset of taking the train in this station, I can assure you that one of these people would have been your friend by now. Only an example or a guide is needed to change and be able to acquire plenty of things, but unfortunately, our silly ego has turned us into insensitive human machines programmed to just produce and make money, only going in one direction just like the rails beneath this train, only moving forward or backwards, without realizing that by taking a small deviation or taking an alternative path, we would find marvelous things that we miss to discover or accept, thus denying ourselves knowledge of their existence and becoming prisoners of our own freedom," concluded the man.

His comment left an impression on me. I totally agreed with him. Life is an enormous outdoor school, with thousands upon thousands of new things to discover, and above all, with something to learn from every day, but since we think we know everything, we deny ourselves the opportunity of knowledge. It is at those moments when the universe acts wisely by placing teachers and tutors along our path so that we can follow their example and learn from them. It reminds us that life is not just about living and dying [or just merely existing], but it is about living to serve and do good and eventually die with the satisfaction of having accomplished what the Supreme Mandate established, leaving an indelible print of our passing in this world.

The caring universe, from which I still had a lot of things to discover, but most of all, to learn from, presented itself to me, via that stranger, to teach me that life does not only go in one direction alone. I made me realize that there are a plenty of alternative paths and detours. Perhaps those detours are not always the easiest ones to take, but they are the ones that lead to big rewards in the end, reminding us that what is good never comes easy, and that all that is easy lasts as long as a heartbeat.

The courteous gesture that I showed that morning made me break the invisible barrier that I myself had created. It hindered me from seeing the world two feet from my nose. The matter of seconds that it took me to do what was right helped me expand my social circle of friends. The people that I've been sharing this train with for years, whom my distrust and insecurity made me see as simple walking numbers, became my friends, thanks to those mere seconds it took me to manifest my courtesy. From inherited in enormous amounts. It is only a question of exporting them and letting them show.

With exaggerated punctuality, a virtue of this city, the train arrived at the station exactly at five past seven in the morning (its established schedule of arrival is every five minutes). For thousands of people like me, the train is our means of safe and practical mode of transportation to get to any destination, saving us from the terrible headache of attempting (in vain) to escape the ugly gridlock during rush hour in each of the highways and expressways of the city. A lot of them are provoked by distracted or irresponsible drivers in their eagerness to beat the time.

As if being a disobedient and rebellious adolescent with raging hormones, I ignored several orders that morning orders which, for years, routine had imposed upon me. Walking a few more meters ahead, I got on to another wagon, totally different from the one I would take every morning. Making my rebellion even more pronounced, I decided to travel standing up, even though there were a few seats available. It was then when I finally saw The Capital of The World and its marvels through the train window; places which I, otherwise, only saw in movies even though I lived in this great city.

Despite being very familiar with the train, changing wagons made me feel like a stranger in my own house, but at the same time, it satisfied me because I was able to take another important step in coming out of my invisible shell that covered me completely. Through change, I was able to help myself find total freedom. It was a vivid contrast to how I saw the world before. I used to have a very limited view of the world, without realizing that it had no limits. Limits do not actually exist. We are the ones who create and decide how far we want to go. We decide whether we want to lead or remain stuck, looking at the rest go by, and to conform to being simple followers. Special and great things are often found within what may appear as very small and insignificant, which we often trip into (but ignore) because of their simplicity, without knowing that with aggression and determination, we can make them grand.

The stare of the other passengers with us on the train were focused on me yet again. Everyone was acting as if they were seeing a ghost or as if I was doing a monologue or an exorcism rite. Different from other occasions, I simply ignored them after greeting them and I couldn't care any less if they kept staring at me. On the contrary, I transformed my head into an invisible vacuum, ordering each of my neurons to absorb every word my friend was saying, because he began to narrate his story that my addicted curiosity anxiously waited for, and I did not want to miss a single detail.

In every stop the train made, I could only notice people getting on and off. I was incapable of observing where their weird stares were aiming at or if they were still talking about me. All of my attention was focused on every single word that my friend spoke, so much so that for a brief moment, I wished the train would take longer in reaching my destination. Each of my neurons, as if obedient children, accomplished the demand given to them, capturing every word my friend was saying and ingraining it in the most secure place in my head, and along with it, foretold another night of intense sleeplessness.

The persistent curiosity in knowing the rest of the story that my strange friend began to continue took my mind to the nirvana of concentration, so much so that it made me lose notion of time and made me forget where I was going. Thanks to my subconscious, which was still held hostage by routine, and assisted by the train crew, I was able to perceive the arrival of the stop at Forty Second Street in Times Square. I was reminded of my destination as if in a session of hypnosis. It helped free my curiosity from the trance it was in, avoiding lengthening my journey.

Snapping out of my trance, I noticed something different: the wagon that we were in was rather full in comparison to the previous days where in it was already empty right before my stop. Mathew's absence was the reason behind it. He was not on board that day to interrupt, disgust people out of the train, and put an end to my friend's story. I asked the strange man with the childish shoes if he knew something about him.

"I thought you were not going to ask about him. I even thought you hadn't noticed that he was not here."

He responded smiling.

"It feels weird not seeing him again. Do you know what's going on with him?"

I asked again.

to get to know the place where several people give their lives and valuable time to serve others without expecting anything in return. Mathew is one of those people." He responded, while inviting me to go and see that place.

"Of course! It would be a pleasure to go see it. That way, I could see what I can contribute for the cause." I responded with sincerity.

"Definitely! The invitation has been given and it's just up to you to let me know when; but it has to be between today and Friday, before I leave this place."

He responded somewhat mysteriously. "Got it, I'll keep that in mind."

I then heard the train crew announce, through loud speaker, that we were about to stop in Thirty Fourth Street, the station where I get off.

Asking him to give my regards to Mathew on my behalf if he saw him and wishing him a good day, I stepped out of the train and headed towards where I work.

"Petition granted! Mathew will surely be happy with your greeting." He responded with a smile, and wished me a good day.

The curiosity in knowing the rest of my friend's story was satisfied upon being assured that my neurons had stored all the intricate details. And as if not curious enough, another mystery dawned upon me and piqued my interest, but this time, I wanted to know where my friend was headed. It was something that I also had to find out.

Holding the rules of the company in due reverence, I arrived at work, not just on time, but rather, early as usual. Thanks to the jokes and tricks that my colleagues never fail to do every morning to begin the day well, and thanks to the work I had already completed the previous day, that day went by like a walk in the park. I finished my journey with the same state of mind in which I began my morning.

Like a flash of a shooting star, I once again found myself sitting on the train. But this time, as I headed back home, I leaned my head on the glass window recalling all of the things that my friend had told me, but above all, the things I did for the first time that morning. At that moment, I made a deal with myself: that I would do the same things again every morning, since it helped me change my way of seeing things and made me feel good having my spirits high.

Taking advantage of that day, when I could leave work earlier than usual, I stopped by my friend Hassan's store as I usually did to say hello and chat with him for a while. As a gift, the universe had given me good energy in my heart and soul that day. My face reflected my state of total happiness and vigor.

"I see you had a good day today!"

My friend Hassan commented, just as I entered his store. "How did you know?" I asked.

"Well, you usually have a long face, except today." He answered as he laughed.

"You're right. It's true, and it's because life has just given birth to a totally renewed adult baby, and that's me."

I told him as I laughed loudly.

"I see that you're regaining your sense of humor. That's good, *you know!* Laughing and feeling good about yourself help maintain a youthful spirit in you. It is then reflected on the exterior, making it more difficult for the years to deteriorate your skin. In my country, after giving thanks to the heavens every morning, for adding one more day to our life, we always practice a bit of laughter therapy to begin the day right. Despite the differences in culture and the fast paced rhythm of this country, I always try to practice that same therapy to maintain control and subtleness in dealing with grumpy customers who come to the store," pointed out my friend, Hassan, with a smile, advising me to do the same.

"For sure, man. My days will not return to being the bitter coffee I was used to drinking. As of today, I have decided to add some sugar so that it will taste better." I responded, and he concluded by saying:

"Well said! And if you don't have anything to laugh about, laugh about yourself. That helps strengthen trust and assurance. Above all, it helps transmit good vibes to other people."

The chat with my friend, Hassan, seemed like an afternoon soiree of well heeled women from distinguished societies, that after their usual tea, they are forced to forget their compulsory glamour and become judges and authorities of fashion, righteously criticizing their absent friends, neighbors, and the rest of society. Nothing escapes them, erroneously believing that only they have ascended to the throne of perfection. But and there was always something to learn day by day from all the things that were happening.

After a long day and a deserving and productive chat with my friend, Hassan, I decided to walk back home, but not before kidding around that the city would have two new millionaires very soon. It would be the best Christmas gift ever. We decided to give a last push of luck to our lottery ticket, hoping to win at least the minimum part of the jackpot, which was precisely what was being played that night.

Whether I won the lottery or not, it really didn't matter to me anymore. I moved it as a secondary plan in my life. In stark contrast to getting millions of green rectangular papers that can only buy a passing and false state of happiness, my new way of seeing life presented me with something more priceless but overall, eternal.

Despite how cold the afternoon was, I took my time in getting home, breaking the chain of stressful and fast paced walk I would otherwise do.

Once at home, after finishing all the chores, sharing a pleasant moments with my roommates, and filling myself with enough coffee to offset sleep and keep me awake, I locked myself in the hollow silence of my bedroom, confirming once again that silence is a thinker's best friend.

Once inside my room and after getting comfortable, I left the soft and gentle light of the lamp, next to my bed on and I sat in front of my computer, taking my first sip of coffee, I began to continue the story that my greed demanded to know, starting with the last line I left hanging the night before.

"So what did you feel when Lucas and William hugged you once they knew you were leaving?" I asked my new friend.

That question opened the door for him to continue his story, and for me to continue writing this piece of literature that took a toll on my sleep yet again for the third night in a row.

He kindly asked me to pay attention; and taking all the time in the world to give me a very extensive answer, he responded:

"The tight hug that I received from Lucas and William reminded me of that special hug that I received from my precious daughter and family at the moment of my departure. It was a hug that stayed ingrained in my skin and in the most intimate and sheltered part of my memories. Knowing that in a couple days, the strong ties which developed in such a short amount of time between the children and I would be broken, made me sink into an inconsolable storm of loneliness. Cenelia, who was for the kids, their adorable and protective "*fairy godmother,*" and for me, the most exceptional woman with a heart that exemplified goodness, generosity, and love, also approached me to give me a very tight hug.

The universe, in compensating for my crossing, my long hours of loneliness, and my family, who against my will, I had to leave behind, gave me a new family in another distinct and distant land. It showed me that borders, social classes, religion and any other type of prejudice do not exist. They only exist in our minds. Ironically, we have created all of these to cause a division amongst ourselves, knowing deep inside that we are all the same. Social classes, economic positions, religion, or skin color, do not change the miracle that we all have blood flowing through our veins. Perhaps social and economic classes determine difference and inequality, but this difference is superficial and shallow, because underneath our skin, we are all completely the same, with no differences among us whatsoever." "Don't you think?" asked the stranger, who was becoming less of a stranger, because his story demonstrated that he was a man with a great heart, as reflected in each of his words.

After he penetrated my heart and soul to the deepest core with those words, he continued his story:

"Reminding everyone that it was a celebratory moment and not a time for mourning, I suggested to Lucas and William to take Cenelia for a ride around the city. Because of her illness, it had been a long time since she was able to go out of the house, and she definitely deserved a tour. She was a queen that night and we needed to treat her as such, pleasing her in everything. It was also some kind of a family outing, because even Charlie was with us. We left the restaurant and walked to a park across the street. We came across a horse carriage terminal. The owners offered tourists a reasonable price for a night ride through the most spectacular parts of the city. Our queen and William got in one carriage, while Lucas, Charlie, and I got in another. Thus we began our ride. As I observed the magnificent city, I couldn't help but feel fortunate for all the good things

After a long ride with various stops in beautiful sites of the city, we decided to take our queen back to our palace. Her loyal subjects had to rest because a long day of work awaited us, and we had to be ready to transmit our lively energy to our demanding audience. After giving me and the kids a hug of gratitude, Cenelia went to her room to rest. Different from always being the first ones to go to bed, Lucas and William stayed and chatted with me for a while longer. Lucas made sure Cenelia was sleeping. He came near me and made me promise that what he was about to say would be a secret between us three. They asked me to take them with me to the city where their mother was supposedly working. Once there, they would look for her and ask her to come back home with them and with their adorable Cenelia. There was really no more reason for her to work as hard and as far away since they already had a bike. I confess that their petition took me by surprise. It left me speechless for a few moments and rendered me in a crossroad, for I did not want to hurt them. I thought for a moment, and finally told them that it was not convenient to talk about this topic in the house, and that it would be better to wait and talk about it at work the following day, because perhaps Cenelia could hear us. It was enough to cripple my mind. It was as if I was poured with a cold bucket of water, plunging me in very long night of wakefulness, tossing and turning, wondering what on earth I could possibly tell them. The truth was: in whatever manner I tell them, it would still turn out to be very complicated.

I did not want to bear the guilt of causing Cenelia anguish and pain by separating her two little ones away from her. Obviously, I was not irresponsible enough to take them with me secretly and leave them alone in a strange new place where no one could protect them. That was the reason I decided to leave secretly. I knew they would be mad at me, but it was the most sensible and correct thing to do. From too much thinking, my neurons ended up in a cemetery somewhere inside my brain, and it impeded me from falling into Morpheus' arms, making my sleeplessness that night even more tragic.

The love that Lucas and William had for their mother was so big that it made them ignore the danger that they could expose themselves into by going out and looking for her. Although I wanted to help them, it was going to be a very complicated task. Firstly, because I was in a country that was not mine. I barely knew the city in which I was staying, and secondly, no one really knew the whereabouts of their mother. The city that Cenelia told them was just a part of the tale, thus there was no exact information regarding her whereabouts.

After everything they did for me, and how well they treated me, it was not right that I just left unceremoniously, but I had no other choice. It was either that, or being the one to blame for all the crying and sadness, not only for Cenelia, but also for my two little teachers. The neurons that I sacrificed that night died a horrible death in trying to help me elaborate a plan which consisted of making them believe that I was going to take them with me. Once that happened, I would wait until everyone was asleep and without hesitation or looking back, leave silently in the stillness of night. Taking advantage of my sleeplessness, I prepared and left my suitcase ready, and finally, I waited for zero hour to execute my plan.

Making unnecessary toss and turns, unable to catch a wink of sleep, and tired of listening to Charlie snore who slept like a baby, I watched the first ray of light seep in through a hole in the ceiling. I got up and went to receive the morning outside the house. I took that opportunity to walk and take a deep breath, hoping to decrease my tension. Lucas and William were stunned when they could no longer find me in the house. They called Cenelia and they came out to look for me. When they found me, I saw a sign of relief and happiness on their faces, and that was how I confirmed how hard my departure would be for them.

The tension that I wanted to dissipate by walking around the house, and the several deep breaths of fresh morning air that I took repeatedly, was distressed with Lucas and William's insistence of going with me. Putting the first phase of the plan into action, I made them believe that I was going to take them with me. By doing so, I was able to appease their impatience of wanting to begin the adventure, for a while. Cenelia, who was not a dumb woman, and showing that the white on her hair was not in vain, perceived something rather unusual in my state of emotion; she asked me if I was feeling fine.

"Oh I am. It's probably because of the tension of having to travel again." I responded with anguish.

the relaxing exercises that I did before leaving the house helped me lower my terrible anxiety. To top it off, as if it was by coincidence or they were really waiting to follow my plan, Lucas and William had gone ahead of me and had prepared a suitcase, planning everything for their supposed trip with me. On the way to our place of work, Lucas very excitedly let me in on his plan, totally ignoring the risk that it represented for them. He assured me that it would only take days to go and bring their mother back, emphasizing how Cenelia would not worry so much about them. I learned great lessons from my two little teachers with each day that passed. Their innocence, but above all, the love they felt for the person who gave them life, made them the perfect example of forgiveness and sacrifice. I am a hundred percent sure that even if they knew their mother had abandoned them, they would still love her and would still go out and look for her, just as they wanted to do now, without caring about the consequences. It was because innocent hearts had no room for negative feelings.

The universe reminded me again that there really are instances or moments beyond or will or control. As if the surprises were not enough, before closing our last show, the two toddlers had another surprise for me: the most important and special one in my entire life, one that changed my plans to travel yet again and made my stay in The City of Eternal Spring even longer; but above all, one that made me change my life completely, and forever.

Regardless of my disoriented mood and low note, we were able to open our first show with great success, adding another day to our good luck. After each show that started and ended, the tension and worry that I had gradually disappeared. But during the recess of our last show, we rested and decided to have a drink and discuss the final details of our stellar show, when something similar that happened to me when I was thirteen took place: my heart inexplicably accelerated to a thousand beats per second and my nerves took a hold of me. My entire body was transformed into a fragile leaf that shook to a minimum breeze. My heart and soul, perhaps connected directly with universal and spiritual forces, began to feel the arrival of something emotional. I didn't know if it was good or bad, but it was an inexplicable feeling of anxiety.

Punctual as always, our stellar performance started at exactly six o'clock. At that moment, anxiety and nervousness had overcome me completely. This was coupled with the idea that permeated in my head of sneaking out; it made me fall into the height of errs. Fortunately, Lucas and William, who were already experts in the art of improvisation, majestically saved my reputation in front of the crowd. With my heart beating fast, and my nerves having a feast in my body, they made me feel a very bizarre sensation. I knew that it was not stage fright since I was already accustomed to be in front of an audience. The creator of that special sensation appeared in front of that entire sea of faces. It was a bit before our rendition of a song I had composed for Lucas and William, which had become an artistic staple of each one of our shows. She had a small birthmark on her mouth, a charming smile and the most beautiful face that my eyes had ever seen. I don't know if it was chance, coincidence or if she was there fulfilling destiny's disposition, but regardless of the reason, a few meters away from me was the most beautiful woman that my eyes had ever seen. She was just as I had dreamed her.

After having traveled many years in the express lane of loneliness that ran at an unlimited speed through the highway of time in an accelerated and wild way. Suddenly, on an afternoon in November, it came to a surprising halt and it indicated that I was no longer a passenger in that express lane and it asked me to get off. Destiny left in the middle of my road a beautiful look and charming smile, which were responsible for my new route. She was amongst the crowd and in front of me applauding our act; it was just as I had pictured it. To many this was simply the love of their lives, I dared to go further and call her: my soul mate, my other half, the perfect gift that any man dreams of. I believed that we simply needed to meet, because it was written in heaven that she would be mine and I would be hers. Perhaps this sounds like an exaggeration, but anyone who has ever truly fallen in love knows what I'm talking about. One night in November, after the day was dying, a simple look was also making my loneliness perish. At that moment I knew that life had given me another chance to be happy, but specially to live once again.

Very nervous and trembling, I looked at her straight in the eyes, pretending to give the impression that I had known her for an entire was one of the most special of my entire life. Regardless of having had certain experience in matters of love, never before had I felt something so special and grandiose as to what I felt that time. Ever since that day, I learned that there are certain loves that even if they are important, they leave without a trace, and there are others that come only once but change us completely. There was no simple logic for that event; I was convinced that she was what I had been waiting for my entire life. It was merely one look that completely changed my entire world. And it was strangest because regardless of knowing nothing about her, not even her name, I already felt that I loved her. It was so easy to fall in love with her, that if love exists after death, I would doubtlessly fall in love with her and love her with the same intensity that I did for the first time.

She reacted to our performance with several applauses and some money; however, she mysteriously disappeared amongst the crowd, leaving me with the desire of talking to her and knowing who she was. But, overall, she left me with the great uncertainty of not knowing if I would ever see her again. The worry and tension that I had completely disappeared with the image of that beautiful woman that began to overcome every part of my head. So much so that Lucas assured me that I was the child here and reminded me that it was time to go home. He made me step down from the cloud that that beautiful face made me climb. With the appearance of that being that moved me, and perhaps my only chance to meet the person that would make me the happiest in love, I didn't know whether to go forward with my plan to leave or wait for the following day to see if she once again appeared in the audience. From that moment, indecisions were ubiquitous and turned my head into a battlefield.

At times I felt as if life had given me what I deserved; aside from having giving me a family and a wonderful daughter, it was giving me that opportunity to meet someone special in my life. Only a few minutes of her magic were able to change everything surrounding me, and for my mood, which was on the ground, to rise as helium balloons as high as the sky. The children, who had no knowledge of romantic love, looked at the idiotic face I had acquired; they made fun of me nearly throughout my entire return home. But it didn't bother me in least possible way. To a certain extent, I shared smiles with them because I also mocked how stupid we adults become when it comes to being smitten or in love. What they didn't count on was that sooner or later, that stage of infatuation would also surprise them.

When we got home, Charlie came out to greet us. I embraced him with my arms and hugged him in a way that corresponds to his joy and unconditional care with which he always received us. Taking advantage that we were all seated around the table, I told Cenelia what happened and sharing my happiness, she wisely advised me to listen to my heart, that she is the most suitable person to help make the most adequate decision. She reminded me that she supported my decision and was glad because that meant that I would be with them longer. After having dinner, and cleaning up the kitchen and the house, Lucas and William asked me to teach them how to ride their bicycle. We went around the house laughing and making fun of the falls. Underneath it all, I was still worried because they took advantage of any opportunity to remind me of our famous trip and I couldn't think of anything else, but to tell them that we had to wait until the following day to do it. They were completely convinced of my word, calmed down and were dedicated to maintain the equilibrium of the bicycle. I on the other hand, sat down to play with Charlie, trying to dissipate my tension in something else.

As the hours passed, the hope of my little masters of finding their mother was growing more and more. On the contrary, the anxiety and the indecision were beginning to overpower me by not knowing whether to wait or to execute the said plan. Doing as planned, I had to travel to the country that connects the Pacific and the Atlantic [Panama] to meet with the group of people that, along with me, were waiting for the clandestine guides; people that were bringing illegal tickets to the north. The problem was not whether I stayed or not another day, the problem was that the children were willing at any cost or way to travel with me and I did not want to expose them to the eminent danger that involved taking that trip. When I thought I had everything under control, suddenly I felt I was in the thorns of a dilemma. I was lost in the labyrinth of my own indecisions. At times I wanted to wait for everyone to be asleep, take my things and leave just as I had planned. But at the same time there was something in to be with them so they could take a ride together. Every time that my little masters talked about their mother, it was a direct blow to my heart, a blow that made me feel guilty and impotent by not being able to help them with the search for their mother. The world had me ready for tests and more tests. Many times I was at the verge of giving up, sitting in a corner and waiting for time to consume me. But doing this would only confirm that fear is the refuge of every coward. I, being a man that does not easily give up, armed myself with valor, closed myself in the silence of the night and followed Cenelia's wise advice. I made the decision to stay for one more day, deciding that if I once again saw the woman that overtook my thoughts in such a short period of time, my stay would be indefinite.

The greatest things in life come unannounced at the moment we least expect it, but nevertheless they are accompanied with a great sacrifice. In one corner, the luggage that would sail new routes was ready, and in the other, the women who had illuminated my heart like no one had ever done before. It was a truly important and definitive decision. After several hours of deliberations while staring at the ceiling, and finally remembering the advices from Cenelia, I decided to prolong my visit in that city and patiently wait for my true love. It was a difficult battle because leaving was my last objective, but after much reflection I came to the conclusion that if it was a call from destiny it didn't have to make things more difficult.

With the decision made, the tranquility and the peace that I had not felt for a long time came with the image of that beautiful look that had overwhelmed my head. Thinking about her made me realize that the decision I had made was the most successful and that the sacrifice was worth it. After that I didn't know anything; the sleepless hours coupled with the image of that beautiful face, sequestering all of my thoughts, took me directly to the arms of Morpheus; as if I was a baby, it locked me in his dreams, compensating for all the hours of insomnia that I had gone though.

At the end of dawn, Lucas got up as if he was the captain of a military regiment, announcing that we were late for work. To my regret, he interrupted the sweetest dreams that not even the delicious smell of Cenelia's coffee was able to wake me. With Luca's loud voice, there was no remedy but to stand up and receive any scolding. But the clock, contrary to Lucas' impatience that morning, granted me a few more minutes to get ready.

After having breakfast, I was ready to once again start a new work day; a day of decisions and also a special one, because from the moment that I opened my eyes and stood up on the floor, I knew that it was not going to be an ordinary day. It would be important for all the events that marked my destiny. I wanted to see her so bad that in my head there was nothing more than her. From the instant that we arrived at the work site, a maddening anxiety flowered, since at any moment she could appear; therefore, I couldn't concentrate a hundred percent in what I needed to do. At each hour that the clock marked, I was growing mad by not seeing her, and before our last show, my hopes were agonizing; hence, I thought that it was best to calm my anxiety, put my impatience aside and concentrate in what I needed to do for things to turn out fine. Besides, if she were part of my life, I would let destiny do its job, whilst I would patiently wait. After setting up our show and laughing for a moment, we were once again starting our last show that was becoming more popular each day. While my little colleagues did their part in the show, my eyes were posted on the crowd, trying to find those bewitching eyes that were stuck in my head. But as much as I checked and rechecked many times, I could not find those brilliant eyes. This produced a small burning in my stomach, but I immediately remembered that I needed to be strong and responsible with my work.

Shortly before closing our final show, I asked Lucas and William to be seated next to me to perform together the song that I had composed for them and which we used to close every show. Thinking that it would be my last performance and farewell, I sung it with a lot of heart and melancholy. Such was my performance that it produced a sea of tears. The kids looked at me with an expression of confusion, they could not understand why I cried and I finally infected them with melancholy. Tears ran through their cheeks from the great care they had acquired for me, and in some pure way they accompanied me in a pain they had no idea of. Who says that men don't cry? If crying doesn't make us less men or cowards, on the contrary, crying is necessary for men because it's how we shake off that deprivation to the emotional. It is how we demonstrate that we are not made out of and all other stupid things that fill us with prejudices, we are able to create a strong friendship tie. That afternoon we lowered the curtain of our stellar show, making us receive the most sumptuous ovations from the public. I thought that only Broadway artists were worth of such acclamations, but I noticed that what people most value is work done from the heart, and this moves anyone.

Having finished the show and playing my last card, I made a panoramic look towards the agglomeration of people, and with this failed attempt I lowered my head as a sign of resignation. I took advantage of the moment when the kids collected the money, I took out my suitcase and I camouflaged myself into the crowd so that they would not notice my departure. As I was walking through the crowd, I suddenly felt that someone touched my shoulder. I was motionless for a few instances and with my heart about to burst. In reality, I didn't want to turn back and see because I did not want to fail in the illusion that it was not she. But I armed myself with courage, and slowly turned until her beautiful big and bright eyes illuminated my face. She had been there for some time, but perhaps my anxiety did not allow me to see her. Jonathan, her younger brother, who would later turn into one of my best friends, accompanied her.

Turning my desire to hug her into a greeting with hands, which were inevitably covered in sweat, I told her that I was very glad to see her again, and she told me the same with a slightly timid, but charming smile. I dared to once again grab her hand and take her to Lucas and William. Lucas, who was the most burlesque, made a comment about being a pleasure to meet the woman who had me disoriented and with a foolish face. William, on the other hand, starred at her, contemplating her beauty and greeted her calmly.

Once the show was over, the crowd left the theater and there was a bit more privacy. The kids cleverly entertained Jonathan with their juggling and magic tricks, in such a way that her and I were alone, face to face. We sat on a platform to chat and at that moment where time didn't matter, I learned her name and part of her life. Her name was Claudia, a name that resonates in my mind and heart forever.

"Hello, how are you? Do you remember me?" Asked Claudia.

"How could I forget, if I couldn't stop looking at you yesterday." I answered a bit nervous and perhaps excited.

Then, with a bit of audacity, I delved into chance with what she could answer, and daringly said:

"You know? I have fallen in love with you; I have to admit it. I only hope that the brightness in your eyes when you look at me is a sign of reciprocated love."

With an exquisite smile she looked straight at my eyes and with a lot of confidence she said:

"Well, you have nothing to worry about because you are totally countered; I feel for you what you feel for me"

When hearing those words, an adrenaline discharge ran through my body; waking the butterflies that were asleep in my stomach for years. When seeing that cupid's magic was beginning to act between us, I took her hand and through a kiss I placed my life and soul in her hands; a kiss that one hundred percent reciprocated, with the same love and the same passion that I gave her; a kiss that touched my soul, and a kiss that was the beginning of a wonderful love story.

I don't know if it was by chance or simply because destiny wanted it this way, but my years long dream had become a reality, since I was sure that she was my soul mate, the perfect complement, the ideal partner. She was a miracle made into a woman, which I desired to find my entire life. And at certain moments I even thought that we were the reincarnation of a great love from the past, a love that promised to love each other infinitely. I say it for the great connection that was between us, it could be said that we belonged to one another; she was made for me and I, for her. That simple.

After sharing that magical moment that transported me to heaven, Claudia promised me that we would see each other the following day and she left, giving me a passion flavored kiss, like fruit and flower as well; a kiss that left me thinking about her for the rest of my days. Every time that I remember that moment, I think about her and my soul becomes serene and light.

I had always become the attentive ear to great love stories, and now I had become one of the protagonists. I no longer dreamt in silence, longing for someone to come to my life. Now I was the narrator of my own love able to avoid for it to happen. Perhaps for that reason the spiritual forces permeated my expectations and patience with the arrival of that wonderful woman, and for her presence to put an end to my accustomed and ceaseless loneliness.

Reminded then that words are worth more than any signed contract, hence, I began to fulfill the promise I had made to myself. On our way back home, before Lucas and William mentioned the trip that lay ahead, I gave them the news that my stay in their house would be prolonged. They were slightly surprised, but at the same time excited. They were filled with joy and began to jump in the bus that was taking us home. In order to not kill the hopes that they had to look for their mother, I told them that I would stay longer with them and think of a good plan, become assure of her whereabouts and look for her. They thought that it was a good idea. Lucas, as leader of the group, told me that if I wanted to stay longer I needed a stage name, since this would give my character more prestige; this was already a condition to continue working with them. Shrieking with laughter he made it clear that I would be the clown *"cantarín"*. I showed no objection and accepted his decision. In fact, that name was comical to me and even childish and it fitted my personality. That day I not only found the love of my life, I had also been baptized with an artistic name, but most importantly was my initiation as another member of Lucas' family.

When Cenelia learned of the news, she laughed and said that since she was clairvoyant, she knew that I would stay with them. She then said that we needed to celebrate, gave me a motherly hug and reminded me that I was part of her family and invited us to sit down for dinner. I don't know if it was intuition or because she really was clairvoyant and could see what was going to happen to me, but she put a lot of effort on the dinner that included a small cake made with her own hands. With the butterflies were once again awake, moving around my stomach, with the excitement and feelings having a feast in me, I felt as if there were enough reasons for that celebration.

At the time that Cenelia served a piece of that delicious cake, I was impressed once more, because she made a chocolate one, which is my favorite. I stood and stared at the cake and I took the spoonful thinking that Cenelia was very bold, or it was a simple coincidence to have made my favorite cake. Anyway, I continued enjoying the moment. It was difficult to believe that all those wonderful things came at once. At times I felt as if I didn't deserve them, but if they happened this way it was because life had given me the opportunity to laugh again, and I laughed once again. I don't believe that it was merely a whim. Undoubtedly, the many prayers that my mother, daughter and entire family raised to heaven pleading for me had been made effective. Perhaps, I also made it possible for things to turn this way with each one of my sacrifices and well made decisions. For my happiness to be one hundred percent complete, only my main and inbred family was needed; meaning my parents, brothers, little nephews, and especially my loving and charming baby that was the strength of all my days. Each day that I was apart from them, the need for them made me miss them even more. But thanks to friendship, the witticism of Lucas and William and the unconditional care of Cenelia, the sorrow of being apart from them was less painful. By knowing that the political condition of the country was stabilizing once again, gradually the communication with my family was made constant. We took advantage of every medium possible to greatly minimize the distance between them and I. The laws that the universe establishes are very clear: it is not possible to have it all at the same time and true happiness is coupled with sacrifice.

After dinner, Cenelia told me that she would like to see my country one day and asked me talk about my family. To talk about my family would take a long time, but I will be brief, I told her while smiling. We are relatively small family; we are three brothers, I am the oldest and a single father of a beautiful four years old girl who is my reason for living. My brother, Luis, the middle child, who's lived in Europe for several years; and my little sister Lucy who we lovingly call Lulú, is the youngest. She lives with my mother. My father passed away a few months ago. I told her this in a very general way as I was making a cordial invitation to visit my country whenever she wanted. She once again reminded me that I could count on them, that that was also my home and they my second family.

Once the dinner and the cleaning up was over, we sat down to chat for a moment. Lucas and William who appeared as finance experts, gave Cenelia a vast amount of money her to save, which we had been able to was slowly growing and it was thought to go exclusively for the education of the children. For my part, abiding by my obligation I did exactly the same. In spite of her refusal to accept my money, I gave it to her insisting that my stay would be indefinite and it didn't seem fair that only my little masters would cover all the costs.

While Cenelia went to put the money away, Lucas whispered in my ear that they were going to visit their friend Mickey, the old oak tree that guarded their treasure. He then asked me to accompany them, arguing that it was good to leave the crowd miss them a little and wait for them to reload their pockets. He was saying that they will take the next day off, and this seemed perfect to me. But suddenly I remember that I had had an important date and needed to return to our place of work, this time not as an actor, but as a transient man in love. I was dying for the next day to come and to be six in the afternoon to once again see the woman that had occupied my dreams. However, many hours were needed for this to come so I needed to take it easy.

After a moment of unforgettable celebration everyone went to sleep. I stayed with Charlie sharing our accustomed couch. That night I let him chose the best side because I had always taken the best part, and it didn't seem fair with my poor friend; also, I felt giving because I was in love and nothing seemed to bother me. So, without any pressure whatsoever, much more relaxed, I was able to fall asleep; simply waiting for the hours to pass and for the clock to dial six in the afternoon so I could go to my encounter with my romantic date.

The image of my new love completely overtook my dreams and like a powerful sleeping aid, it made me fall into the most profound and comforting sleep. That moment belonged to me so much that not even the strongest of the earthquakes would have awakened me. Evidently, that night's celebration exhausted all of us a lot that it extended our sleep more hours than what we were accustomed to. The first to wake up, as always, was Charlie whose sticky kisses and insistence to scratch the door to fulfill nature's call, put an end to my sleep. At that moment it was past nine in the morning and the day was spectacular, with a shining sun to partake in any type of activity. But neither the noise that Charlie made by scratching the door, nor the one that I made when I got up, was able to get the rest to wake up. There was no sign of Cenelia, Lucas and William. In order to not interrupt their rest, I went out with Charlie to buy breakfast from a food stand that was considerably far from the house. This would give them time to wake up on their own. When I returned they were still asleep, so I abused my confidence a bit and seeing that there were things that needed to get done, I began to knock doors and serve breakfast. The first one to get up was Cenelia, followed by Lucas, whilst the little sleepyhead, William, remained battling Morpheus for a while longer. I don't blame him, it was our day off and it was necessary to somewhat recuperate all the hours of sleep robbed from the dawns of work.

After a patient wait, we had to take William from the hands of Morpheus, because nothing woke him up. We were now ready to start our secret adventure. As always, Lucas gave me his small notebook, which contained the balances of his fortune, to put away. After receiving the usual kiss and hug form Cenelia, we started our walk towards the secret place. Charlie, who is a very smart dog, before seeing us leave, sat down and gave us the look of a sickly cat, which was able to persuade us; therefore, we brought him with us, but he did a great job as a tourist guide and bodyguard, guarding us from whoever followed us. When we arrived, the first thing they did was hug Mickey. That act was a type of symbolic rite, thanking the old oak tree for being the custodian of their money and for protecting it. In reality this appeared very important and meaningful because it was a type of connection between nature and them. Here, there was no unidirectional relationship; it was a feedback process between both parties. Following the procedure from the last time, the children unearthed and took out the small wooden coffer that had the money that was destined for the search of their mother. Taking into account that they were going to be part of my family, and that their problems were also mine, I gave Lucas my part of the money to save in order to contribute to their noble cause. They were very happy because this way they were going to reach quicker the amount that they needed for their awaited trip. They hugged me and infinitely thanked me, and then they once again organized the money and processed to bury the box in the same way that we had found it. With another hug, the kids said goodbye to Mickey and they jokingly

Lucas and William were satisfied for having accomplished what was most important to them, and then they asked me to take a stroll through the city. I looked at the time and noticed that it was still early for my date and I thought that it was a good idea, since I didn't want to stay at home, chewing my nails, looking at the clock until it dialed six in the afternoon. Ultimately, I also knew that it was an excuse for the kids to visit their favorite confectionery and have their well deserved weekly dose of sugar. Like the good friends we were, they would help me a little, so they accompanied me to the park, where our theater was improvised and where I had agreed to have my date with my beautiful and loving Claudia. We all got to the park and as we waited, we played with Charlie a bit, and then I saw her come from afar. It was unmistakable; as she got closer I was delighted to see how the sun shined in her hair and how she walked so placid and beautiful to the beat of my pulse. My anxiety stopped upon her arrival.

That day we chatted for a long while, with a few halfway promises. Seeing how everything was booming, two and a half weeks later I took her home to meet Cenelia, who congratulated me for having by my side such a beautiful woman. She advised me to take care of her, but also to be very careful of falling madly in love; to take it easy. I know what she was telling me was in good faith, but it was too late to apply her advice; from the first time I saw her, I had already deposited my entire love in her, and as I was getting to know her, my heart was becoming more and more dependent; turning me into an uncontrollable addict to the fascinating world of her tender and magical love. Every moment by her side turned into pure magic, every day was a new adventure of invented things by the two of us, and recognized by the two of us. I can daringly be sure that she and I were able to reinvent love; I was willing to do anything for her. If necessary, even die for her love, and she was willing to do the same. It was clear that one could not live without the other. Henceforth, I confirmed that the universe created us to be together and we were there to fulfill that mandate.

On a 24th of December, I discovered for the first time that it was not necessary to die in order to go to heaven. Both of us were madly in love, and with the complicity of the middle of night, we decided for the first time to undress our souls; between her body and mine there wasn't any space even for the air to flow. I loved her with the passion that I had never felt before for any other woman. We loved each other so much that we dissipated everything that was prohibited, but at the same time we invented thousands of new things; having love itself surprised by the great love that we felt for one another. I was her painter, and she was my Mona Lisa that cheered my soul with each smile. With each kiss I discovered heaven in her skin; it was simply heaven made into a woman, and although I was inside of her and I could feel the sweet taste of her kisses and the fresh aroma of her skin, at times it appeared as a dream that was difficult to believe. That dawn we turned our most ardent desire into passion and love at the same time; a love that was sealed in promises of two souls that would be together for eternity. The silence of the night, the white sheets and an old picture hung from the wall were the only witnesses of our love pact.

"I am not perfect, nor a superhero; I am simply a nut that adores and loves you. I would like to put the entire world at your feet. You are my world and I am only what you see"

Lost in the obscurity of her hair, counting the birthmarks that shined in the sky of her body and with my heart in my hands, these were the words that were natural to tell Claudia that morning.

"I don't care"

Claudia told me, crying.

Giving me a tight hug, she promised to always be by my side making me feel extremely strong and important. From the first time she came to my life she became the muse of my inspiration, because she dared to buy my loneliness, paying me with an exorbitant quantity of happiness. Loneliness that as a loyal companion, accompanied me everywhere; sometimes it made me feel as if I was no one and suddenly she came with her smile and love to make me as if I was someone important.

One afternoon in April, after work, on our way back home, a man that was totally defeated and with a terrible sadness got on the bus where Lucas, William and I were and sat in the seat in front of us. When he noticed that we were laughing with much joy, he turned around, and with a soft and slow voice, asked me what the secret to happiness was.

"I don't know the secret to happiness, but I do know that love is a great

"Love is what just killed me. Fortunately you have been granted with love and not with betrayal."

He answered me with his eyes watery and completely destroyed.

Without having the minimal idea of the pain that man was going through, and with the confidence I had in love, I gave him some advice without imagining that a few months later I would be in the same situation as him. The advice I gave him I would later not know how to apply them to my favor.

Just as hours elapse on a clock, the days in a month and months in a years, that's how our love elapsed, making everyday a reason for celebration. Slowly consolidated amongst the immortal romances of great transcendence, marking that it would firmly and solidly arrive to our first anniversary, with the promise that we would together let time paint our heads white, for all the promises and thousands of plans that we daily made; our first anniversary would be the most important one of our lives. Well, at least it was going to be important to me.

Blessed is the love of those who decided to procreate you, blessed is the womb that turned that love into a work of art. But even more blessed is the heavenly artist who sculpted you, to make your curves and your anatomy perfect, giving inspiration to my life in every aspect.

Blessed is the life that gave me eyes to see and contemplate you, hands to feel and caress you, and a heart to love and adore you.

Woman, you are not only the desire and skin that I've been dreaming; you are the miracle of life that lives in your being. Woman, you are not only tenderness and passion, you are my infinite peace, my fascination.

Woman, you are not only delirium and love, you are my healing, my medicine from up above. Blessed is the time and the day you were born, but even more blessed is the day you came to me and ended my earthly scorn.

Blessed is the fate that helped me find you, and blessed is your soul, that allowed me to be a part of you. A lifetime wouldn't be enough to love and adore you.

One Friday, tenth of October, minutes before closing our stellar show, as part of my gift for being one more year of my life to her wonderful existence, those were the precise words that came out of my mouth for her; propelled by my heart and born out of my most profound inspiration. It was one of the many dumb and insignificant things that I did for her, but always with my soul. Her sincerity and security of her love for me were the platform that elevated me to the highest point of heaven itself.

Days later, with the permission of Lucas, I turned our place of work into a portal of free access, with the only intention of having the entire world to find out, and also be a witness of, the great love that I felt for Claudia. A portal that, at the same time, turned into an accomplice to all of our follies and as a resource to express, through a few written lines with ink from my heart, the eternal love that I felt for her. Her sincerity and her reciprocated love towards me, took me to be convinced one hundred percent that the universe had assigned that woman to be an accomplice of my follies, partner of my loneliness and absolute owner of all my days and my entire life. Through that portal and in front of the entire world, one afternoon in late October, only a few days away from our anniversary, as another sign of my love towards her, opening one by one the doors of my heart and house for her; I asked her to come into my life completely, as it is established by divine and earthly laws. I dreamt so much of sleeping in the warmth and security of her arms, wake up having breakfast with her sweet kisses and fulfilling my promise of my having my seed germinate in her womb.

Her answer to my proposition was trapped in the time between October and November, assuring me that she would free it on the day of our anniversary. From that day, anxiety once again overpowered me once again, and every day that passed was an eternity. I anxiously waited for the day when the calendar would signal our first year together, a year that through all the plans and promises made by each one of us would be the first one in a thousand years.

With the impatience of a child, I waited and calculated whether it would be yes or no, formulating the hypothesis of what my reaction would be towards either answer, but in the bottom of my heat I had hopes that it would be yes. With a red marker I circled the date of our anniversary in the calendar to remind and also torture me, seeing how the events of time slowly brought me near the said response. Each night I would cross the one and or two follies. It came to strengthen as a great family bond in company and protection of our *"fairy godmother"* Cenelia. Eleven months that passed in an incredible whim, eleven months of having arrived to that beautiful city, eleven months that I was away from my family and the eleven most incredible months of my life lived until that point along with Claudia, the owner of my thoughts.

Only five days were in the way of that glorious moment to start a new life and beginning to fulfill our plans and pending promises. Five days that also gave the start to the interminable ordeal of my life. "I love you, we will soon be together and I promise that no one will separate us" were the worlds I heard come out from her mouth on Friday November twentieth. Blindly ignoring that those would be the parting words, my heart turned them into tons of hopes and wishful thinking, allowing me to live for a few more hours. I didn't imagine that that Friday afternoon my life would make three hundred and sixty degree turn.

Thinking that I would see her once more, excited and happy, the next day I returned to my place of work so that she would come, as always, to inspire me with the brightness of her eyes, and with the tenderness of her smile, but I always waited for her applause that cheered me up greatly. It was six thirty and in the midst of the crowd nothing shined, her absence was so notorious without her that there was a small crowd, and what was completely empty from her absence was my heart. I couldn't imagine my existence without her, because from the first moment when she came to my life I was used to her love. So much so, that if she was gone I would simply be like an abandoned child in the desert. After nearly twelve months of being on time to each one of our dates, only five days from our anniversary, it was the first time my dear Claudia shined for her absence.

The thousands of hypotheses that asked why she was absent were eating my brain like hungry termites. The following day I couldn't say that I woke up because my eyes never closed to rest. When I stood up I grabbed a black marker, walked towards the calendar that each day I had marked in red, waiting for the blessed date for the longed "yes", I looked for the date when Claudia had made me feel the uneasiness of her absence and I reviewed thousands of times with anger, desperation and the impotence that I felt for not knowing anything about her.

Waiting to ameliorate the anxiety that I felt in my heart, accompanied by Lucas and William I returned to our place of work like I did every day. Desperately I began to count the hours waiting for six o'clock to see if the owner of my heart would arrive with nightfall. One late Sunday afternoon that gave my heart the first blow that would cause a small wound that would get bigger with the passing of days. By not seeing her and by not having any sign of her, the anxiety that I hoped to calm with her presence overflowed completely, dragging on its path all the wishes and hopes that I had for Claudia to come back. Only two days passed without seeing her and I felt as if everything was collapsing. My heart was extremely altered, just like she had announced her arrival a year earlier. It now warned me of something and not precisely good things.

Only five days from that dreamt of moment that I anxiety had waited. Claudia disappeared from my life in the same way that she mysteriously came one day. She left without saying goodbye, without giving an explanation or a valid reason of why she decided to distance herself from me. With her departure she took my faith and all the hope that I had deposited in her, and worst of all, with her departure she took my entire life. One November afternoon the woman that destiny put on my path to liberate me from my loneliness, she herself was in charge of annihilating my heart, destroying the pact braided in thousands of promises that we both made. Once again, and ironically, she confined me to my loneliness. Worst of all was that this time she left me without any light, without any signal that would guide my life. I was on a trip going nowhere, and worst yet, I now walked moribund and bleeding from the thousands of wounds that she had given me, without giving me time to heal. As if that was the price to pay for having dared to love her without any prevention.

In all my laments and eternal nights of shed tears, I thought that life aside from being wonderful it was also very ironic; one November afternoon was enough to completely change my entire life; one afternoon in November, a year ago, initiated the most special and wonderful moments of my existence, moments that took me to go to heaven itself, living three hundred and sixty days in a magical paradise. But ironically, another without softening my fall. Her unfulfilled promises made that world of illusion and fantasy that I thought sharing with her collapse, burying me in thousands and thousands of tons of debris, indifference and dissolution. That was the other side of the coin that I now lived. The one that caused terrible internal pain, where the only company were memories, a calendar that laughed out loud, it mocked me to my face for having marked it with hopes in each one of its pages, and the one that reminded me every day of that fateful November 25th.

At that moment I understood the pain of that sadness of that moribund man whom I gave advice to one day. I started to laugh and thought: "*I am truly an idiot! Everyone feels like a superhero when they're in glory, but we are completely negligible when we face our own tragedies.*" I was wrong by feeling immune to pain, at that moment I felt too confident and that's why I dared to give him advise, advise that at that moment I didn't know how the hell to apply it. What I wanted was to go back and find that man to tell him that he was right, that love is not only happiness and wonderful moments, but when one throws his life and soul to the wrong person, there is also the risk to mutilate the soul, and not even the biggest over dose of morphine is capable of calming that pain.

Regardless of so much pain, my heart did not want to accept the truth. With the negligible impulse that remained of living, and still with the hope that she would return, and to not disappoint Lucas and William for all the support that they had given me, I went back to work every day for a little over a month to wait for her to return with sun down. I only wanted to find her, have her face to face so she could give me a logical explanation of her disappearance. That's all I asked. But seeing that she would not return, and with my heart on my hand, I decided to wait for her anymore.

Feeling alone and defeated, now without a reason to continue in that city, I decided to carry on with my trip, trying to distance myself from everything that could remind me of her. But not sufficing with the wound she caused by her disappearance, a few days before leaving, one Sunday morning of the following month she appeared. With the chaos that her reappearance caused, I was able to be happy, but she appeared with all the coldness in the world and had come to assure herself of killing me and also bury me in the oblivion of her indifference. "*I ask you to not look for me anymore, I no longer feel love for you, I am going to give myself another chance, find somebody else. I wish you luck,"* were the last damn words with which she gave me the final stab, and without the least amount of pity, after all that I gave and did for her.

Regardless, and in spite of the contradiction, if I had to live through pain like that again, as long as I felt what I felt for her, I would endure it without a doubt. But I know that it is possible to only love with that intensity once, and I had my chance, although not with the ending I had dreamt of. Since then I was dedicated to travel many roads selling loneliness, my loneliness.

Life, being the fair judge that it is, reciprocated to the thousands of prayers that night after night Lucas and William elevated to heaven, this time they rewarded their persistence, they great virtue of knowing how to forgive, their faith and their good behavior. Three days before my departure, they surprisingly knocked the door that was half way open. Charlie, who was a friendly and tame dog, came out moving its tail. William, brought by curiosity came out to see what made Charlie so happy. Surprised and crying with excitement, he screamed:

"It's mom! It's mom!"

He came to the house and called on his brother and to Cenelia screaming. They were overcome with emotion; undoubtedly they agreed to William's petition and went out to receive that surprising visit. They were all together in one hug gave the welcome to the rest of the brothers, who in some way managed to reach Cenelia's house. Lucas, crying to excitement, asked Richard, the older brother, where their mother was that he really wanted to see and hug her.

"Our mother is still working for a bit longer in order to save money and buy us more toys. But she will soon come to see us, so that we're all together."

Richard answered.

"We don't want toys, we want her; please take us to her we want to see her, it's no longer necessary for her work anymore, we can do it for her"

Lucas said, drowning his cry.

Cenelia intervened rapidly, trying to calm down the mood of her adorable little men, she told them:

Showing her incredible powers of persuasion, Cenelia demonstrated why she was their "*fairy godmother*". She was able to calm down Lucas' and William's sadness and desperation, making them realize that it was a time to be happy and not sad. She invited everyone to come inside the house and as gentile and kind as always she started making a succulent breakfast to assuage the hunger of the new visit. With Cenelia's calming words, and with the deal of going to find their mother and bring her back, my little masters began to ask all sorts of questions to their brothers as they were getting to know them.

Thanks to their arrival, at least at this moment, I forgot all the pain and the thousands of thoughts of sadness that haunted me. I said hello to Richard. I greeted him and told him that it was a pleasure to know him and he amicably asked my name and where I was from. Lucas, mockingly imitating my accent, but the charm that only he possessed, answered instead of me. This was a sign that he knew me too well. William, happy with the arrival of his brothers, took out his bike and let them use it. He also showed them his juggling and magic acts to show off a big. With the arrival of the rest of Lucas and William's brothers, the house was filled with joy that morning, and not only the family grew, but also our prestigious clown association.

Lucas, as leader and founder of that association, with an improvised ceremony in the middle of a delicious breakfast, invited his brother to be part of the group. This was a principal fountain of their subsistence and the one that also allowed me to live in that city for a long time. Once the ceremony had ended and the official naming of the new members of the union, and with Cenelia's blessing, we went out with the rest of the group to show them our workplace. Lucas had decided to take his brothers with us so that they could see what it was about, with the idea for them to familiarize themselves with what would be their new employment and what it meant to be a street artist.

Like great honored guests, we sat them in the VIP section and they were surprised and laughing at our craziness. They decided to carefully observe everything we did. A few instances after having witnessed our act, feeling very confident being able to do it, the new members of our group asked Lucas what would be their role in that imaginary theater. After evaluating them, he assigned a role to each one according to their abilities and talent.

Lucas and his brothers were the clear example of the incomprehension and irresponsibility of many that were unjustly robbed of their rights, and obligated to abandon school in order to make a living. Fulfilling with their role of adults that was unjustly assigned to them, they traded their school's homework and well earned hours of play for intense hours of practice with the goal of perfecting their talent and obtain a few coins that would allow them to survive for another day. All in order to please a very demanding public and also tough since it marginalizes them many times.

With the brilliant act of Richard and the rest of the brothers helping to collect the money that the public voluntarily paid for our act; after finishing our stellar act and also ending our day with the new artists, we returned home, somewhat exhausted but happy. Well, in reality only my other colleagues, because even if I pretended the provoked pain by a cataclysm of disillusionment that left me as a gift that beautiful face that robbed my life, I couldn't hide the sadness and pain that I had inside.

Thinking that the new arrival of more children was going to cause some changes in the house, at times I also wondered that I would not only have to battle with Charlie for that old and comfortable couch, but also with the new guests, meaning Lucas' and William's brothers. At times, the pain that I felt was assuaged by small doses of morphine produced by my internal laugh, but thanks to my little masters that never stopped from surprising me, it was not necessary to dispute the right to sleep in that old couch. The faith and hope to once again be with their family, that my little wise masters never lost, made them carefully and silently prepare the residency of the rest of their family in that home.

Cenelia reminded us that it was an occasion to celebrate, she once again put a lot of effort in the dinner and before finishing it, which went much more than usual as a result of the countless undergone adventures narrated by our new guests. Lucas, as always, without losing his good sense of humor, smiled and invited all of his brothers, including me, to go to his room to show them the respective places where they could go to sleep. After having spent a year in that house, it was the first time that I went into his room. At a quick glance, it looked very small, but once inside it he amicably resigned to share with me, and I don't think that he would've changed it for anything.

Helped by their "*fairy godmother*", ingeniously, the landlords distributed very well the space inside the room, placing bunk beds so all their brothers could sleep comfortably, including theirs. They had also assigned a place and a bed for their mother, who was untouchable, because she was the only one who had the right to that space. At that moment, William's tears began to come out from his eyes by seeing that every space was taken by their respective owners, and only their mother was missing to take her place; a place that appeared to be destined to remain cold and abandoned because the body that needed to warm that bed would never arrive. Perhaps they were different situations, but the pain was the same. Seeing William cry, and being unable to control my sorrow through my eyes, I liberated a great tempest that had been originating in my interior, which I had repressed by the dumb idea of not showing weakness. But once again, the patience and Cenelia's love gave an end to Williams' tears and almost to all my colleagues. The only one that did not cry was Richard, but not because of a lack of emotions, rather because he wanted to transmit strength to the rest of his brothers.

Richard waited for everyone to fall asleep, as a way to blow off steam, and asked Cenelia and I for advice; he sat on the kitchen table to chat with us. His great dilemma, which was taking him to the verge of desperation, was whether to tell Lucas and William that their mother would never return. Her role as a mother was doubled, and she placed her romantic life above the well being of her own children. Promising that she would suddenly return and giving the excuse that it would be for their benefit, she left the country with a one way ticket, leaving the rest of her children to depend on their luck. She had left to follow money and naively, as if she hadn't learned her lesson, once again believed the false promises of a man. He was captivated by her beauty and took her with him, put a high price on her beauty and made her work in the oldest profession of the world.

"I know that the pain to not see their mother once again will be strong, but it is better for them to know the truth rather than having them live with the dead hope of seeing her again; worse yet, that they blame heaven for not sending them a sign to go out and search for her, knowing that our own errors are not heaven's fault," said Cenelia, crying and tightly hugging Richard.

After those words, anything I would've said would have been redundant; hence, I also hugged him and sustained the advice that she had just given him, an advice that like any truth would be very painful, but it would be the correct thing to do. Sooner or later, they would find out the truth, even perhaps through sources outside their brother, and then the pain would be more acute.

By being the oldest brother, the task that awaited Richard would not be easy. The well being of all the children would be under his responsibility.

Trying to minimize Lucas' and William's pain, disguising truth with the breach of the either commandment; the next morning, shortly after finishing our weekly visit to Mickey, which would be the last, Richard, armed with courage and with big tears in his eyes, told them the asphyxiating truth about what happened to their mother.

Tenderness and love were principal chemical formulas with which Cenelia fabricated the medicine for the soul, who also through her words, through a kiss or simply a hug, she would daily inject each one of us with tranquility. Richard went from a critical situation to a stable one, thanks to the words of Cenelia. He was now more calm and quiet, and went to sleep in a comfortable and warm place under the roof that would be his new home; after having unjustly spent, along his other brothers, many nights outside, sheltered only by the cold darkness of the night.

Now, under the care of Cenelia, there I was: the most grave patient, with a severe internal hemorrhage as a result of a heart explosion that blew it to a thousand pieces. It was caused by the wrongful personification of a woman that appeared to be unable to do any harm. This was gradually inducing me into a coma with no return.

"The decisions that the heart makes of who to love are not always successful. By being unpredictable it is very difficult to control it and forbid it to love; I know that the wounds from the heart caused by those wrong decisions do not heal from one day to the other, but I know that you're strong and I am sure that you will overcome it soon. I would like

Those were the calming words with which Cenelia was able to sedate me that night, allowing me to partially recuperate my useless lost hours without sleep.

The following morning, Lucas and William, with no clue of what awaited them, woke up very early to coordinate their brothers for each week's secret missions. William, whispering in my ear that it was time to visit Mickey, asked me to get up. Nearly an hour later than what were accustomed to, we decided to start what would be our last secret mission.

Taking the most precautions, as always, and assuring ourselves that no one was following or monitoring us, we arrived to the place where our tree showed all of its grandeur. The organizers of the visit, as if they knew that this would be the final visit that they were going to make, excitedly ran towards it, hugged it and proceeded to give it the routinely protocol greeting; which ostensibly seemed to be very sincere. Then, they proceeded to introduce the rest of their brother who did not know the reason for the visit to that place.

Lucas' and William's brother were surprised by the chat they had with the old oak, and asked one another if my little masters were sane or were beginning to lose their senses, since they were talking to a tree. They were not the first ones to question that. The first time that they took me to that secret place and began to talk to Mickey, I thought the same. But as time passed, and with each visit we made week after week, I also learned to communicate with him, perhaps not out loud, but internally. It perhaps sounds a bit mad, but I can be sure that the four of us had very interesting chats.

In one of the many chats that we had with Mickey, he joked with Lucas one morning shortly before leaving. He asked him the favor to do something to stop the uncontrollable massacre of the green treasure of the world. He also promised to take care and protect the treasure that he had under his dominion, in exchange for him to tell his species to longer assassinate his, since that although they are big and strong, they are defenseless. Lucas, saying goodbye with the accustomed hug promised Mickey to not do anything that would harm him or others from his species.

Lucas' incredible vocation to do what was right, fulfilling the promise that he made to our great friend Mickey, led him to perform a scene in each one of our shows dedicated entirely to the old oak. It consisted of a tree costume made by Cenelia, which William was in charge of wearing as a graphic representation of the piece. He also had a speech that was well pronounced by Lucas and me, where he explained to everyone present what coniferous like those represent to us, and they need to continue on their feet, aging thanks to us. And if they have to die, it has to be by their own account and not by our hands. Lucas' promise was fulfilled. Perhaps our efforts would not stop the indiscriminate cutting of wood, but it would perhaps create consciousness to the people that came to see us, who could also be transmitters that would reach other people.

The creation of the world is not only perfect, but also wonderful. Nothing was created by mere capriciousness. Each living being in this world, along with us human beings, is here fulfilling something that is perfectly planned. With Lucas and William I did not only learn values such as friendship, loyalty, love towards family and towards others, but also love in harmony with living beings that the universe put in this world to be part of its majestic creation.

After a warm hug that Lucas and Williams gave Mickey at the moment that followed unearthing their treasure. Richard grew innate strength to prepare to apply the advice that Cenelia had given him the night before, which seemed to torment him as a result of the face of uneasiness that he had.

"It is not easy for me to tell you this. I know that this will cause you a lot of pain, but it is better for you to know that our mother will no longer be with us. She decided to take a road different from ours and to distance herself forever in spite of the love that we feel for her, nor the pain that her absence causes us. Regardless, we will continue loving her and if she decided to come back one day, we are going to receive her with all of our heart because thanks to her, and the pain of giving us birth, we are alive. From now on I will be in charge of you and I promise that I will never leave you"

Without giving greater details of the disappearance of their mother and following Cenelia's advice, with those words Richard crucified the hope for the children to once again see their progenitor. Lucas, refusing to

His tears gave Mickey's thirsty roots all the water that they needed. He leaned towards a thick cortex so that it would absorb all of his pain, sliding down to its base.

After a short moment of psychological recuperation, towards the situation, Lucas added:

"This is the product of our days of hard work that were going to be used to undertake our search for our mother, but it is useless now since she doesn't love us"

After the aforementioned, he took out all the money that he had inside the box, gave it to Richard and furiously grabbed the defenseless wooden box and threw it several meters away from the pit in which it lay. Burying in its place the hope that they had to see their mother once again; taking with them their crushed hearts, several broken dreams, and a vain effort that they had been working toward. With this, they were not only cancelling their valuable saving account, but also liberating Mickey from the great responsibility of continuing to take care of their treasure. Moreover, they left it guarding the invisible corpses of their faith that lay dead inside that small grave, which they had left open.

In his attempt to comfort the inconsolable, Richard took little William in his arms and picked him up from Mickey's roots; a place where he ended up after the strong impact caused by that heartbreaking news. For my part, preventing the other one of my little masters from drowning in his tempest,

I hugged him and whilst we got on our way back home, I narrated part of a story that my mother used to tell me when I was little. I expected not to completely heal his heart, but at least transmit a small dose of a sedative for his terrible pain.

Breaking the custom that we had of going to the confectionery to fill up with sugar every time that we visited our secret place, that day we arrived home much earlier than usual. They arrived to recover from their pain and I was trying to finish the final details of my trip for the following morning, just as I had them programmed. Like with its tests had hit us hard and equally to the three clowns, perhaps creating distinct feeling, but the intense and tearing pain was the same.

As it was expected, my farewell passed any sentimental scheme as a result of the strong friendship that I had developed with my little masters and by the strong emotional bond that I had developed with Cenelia.

Regardless of not getting to know their other brothers very well, I was also able to appreciate them for how special and charismatic they had been. Very early next morning, with a strong hug of several minutes, receiving her blessing and a good luck kiss for one last time, and promising that I would come back to visit her, I said goodbye to Cenelia. As expected, melancholy began to reign gradually since a special and important stage of my life was being left behind. In spite of Charlie having that old couch to himself, he did not seem very happy with my departure. On one side were the clashes and disputes that we had for the couch; as a pet and master we knew how to maintain a good relationship and there was no room for grudges, so I grabbed him on my arms and hugged him. For his part, he licked my cheeks and said goodbye to me; wishing me good luck I suppose.

That morning, the prestigious group of clowns was left without one of their members. Although my little masters were not with their mother but with the rest of their brothers and Cenelia, I felt a little calm because with them leading, I was sure that they would be fine. Accompanied by my colleagues, as always, I left very early to take what would be our final journey: they headed towards their place of work and I, without having the slightest clue of what awaited me ahead, headed towards the bus terminal in order to continue on my way. My little masters, along with the rest of their brothers, decided to cancel the first two shows in order to accompany me and say goodbye to me, joking around with me for one last time. Regardless of the farewell of my family and friends, that departure was the saddest one of my entire life; an image that remained ingrained in my head for the rest of my days. Accompanied only by a small handbag that was my only luggage, which became my only friend and travel partner, after saying goodbye to my little masters and colleagues, I took bus number fifty one which took me directly to the northern border after almost three and a half days of travel.

Putting in practice the advice "*time and distance cure any pain*", that so many experts in the topic of love profess and regardless of being possible for me to return to my house in order to be with my family, I decided not to do it. On the contrary, I made the decision to distance myself from the creator

As the bus drove off the terminal and began to leave the city, the nostalgia of leaving behind the good moments that I passed along with my little friends, the adventures lived with them and a future along whom I thought would be the woman of my life, gradually empowered my immense sadness, making my vision blurry at times. After an exhausting, but very calm trip, without any major setbacks and easily going through many military outposts in the region, I arrived at a small town close to the border, which was a refuge and stream point for all that traveled the same way I did. Since it was a tropical zone, the heat was unbearable. I believe that the temperature was close to 38 and 40 degrees Celsius. The heat was overwhelming, even in middle of darkness, following the traces left my thousands of travelers that passed daily through that path, guided only by my intuition, entrusted only by my luck on the universe and by a small rabbit foot that Lucas gave me before leaving, I broke through the border of the country that connects the Pacific and the Atlantic [Panama]; exactly eleven thirty at night. As a result of the clandestine identity that I have myself, I was rewarded with various scratches and cuts by going through the dense vegetation, which was the only entrance.

The following morning, breathing the warm tropical climate and putting into practice the geographical knowledge that I had learned in high school, which were corroborated by various people throughout my journey, I was willing to invade each one of the remaining countries that were in the way of the land of Quetzal and I. After a long voyage of fifteen days I reached *Tecun Uman*, a small border town located north of the Quetzal country [Guatemala]. Along with Christian, who I hired the day before his arrival at the capital of his country, so that he could be my clandestine tourist guide, we posed on the banks of a river, hidden between bushes waiting for the sun to finish his day and would go to sleep in order to take advantage of the northern neighboring country.

Until then, I had reached almost the seventy percent of my voyage; the other thirty percent was the hardest. Aside from entrusting it on the universe and on the talisman that Lucas had given me, I felt obligated to entrust it on the clandestine guides: who were owners and dons of the borders. Everyone that entered their dominions, if they were not obligated to contract their services, needed to pay a determined amount of money for only stepping on that lace that they called nobody's land. Along with us, two Asians were there who had also contracted Christian's services since they were looking for a way to reach the same destiny as I.

As we waited sun fall, hidden in the vegetation, we observed each one of the movements by the neighboring border police, which was moving on the other side of the river, guarding for security. This will help us have a clear perspective about what awaits us on the other side. Christian, listening to the signal that was made by one of his contacts on the side of the border, which indicated that there was no security and the area was completely clear, proceeded to take out from the dense vegetation an improvised small boat, which appeared to be built by him, which was his principal work tool. It consisted of two logs of wood, attached by strings to two spare parts of car tires, which permitted floated and were towed by him through a rope tied to his shoulders and chest; shouting that it was time and that we did not have much of it. Between round trips, each one of us was given a tour of the river, which appeared to be very tranquil and calm, but according to comments and stories that were narrated by residents of that zone, it was very dangerous due to its depth and great quantity of eddies that were formed under its tranquil and passive waters. They had swallowed several clandestine travelers that were trying to cross, reminding us that we should not be too confident on tame waters.

Christian proceeded to help cross one by one the Asian women, who were assisted rapidly by one of his contacts on the other side, and also moved them to the hideout. When the two ladies where safe in the other side, he dragged me and I was also helped by Benjamin, the other clandestine guide. Our tour through the river finished at two thirty in the morning, Christian, fulfilling with his part of the pact, left us safe on the other side. From that moment, Benjamin was in charge of us and he would help us move in the country of tequila and nopal [Mexico]. He also kept us in the hideout for almost three hours, until it was completely safe for the border patrol to clear out the zone and take us to a more comfortable and secure place. every centimeter and a majority of the clandestine routes and each of the official movements of the border officials and immigration; it could be said that he had even pacts with them. As a result of the astronomic profits that was very tight in the midst of thick vegetation. Later, he proceeded to take us to take us to his automobile that was parked a few meters from the place where we were hiding. As if we were his luggage, he placed us in the trunk of the car as people who were on the road looked at us. In spite that they were main witnesses of what happened daily in that place, no one dared to talk about it or much less give them away. All those people were a circle that had complete control of that place, the warning in part of the clandestine guides for the whistleblowers was very clear.

In spite of being like sardines in a can, I felt privileged of being trapped in the middle of the exotic beauty of two beautiful women. Perhaps not in the most conventional way, but it could be said that I fulfilled the fantasy dreamt of many men.

After an uncomfortable trip that lasted around an hour, we arrived at Benjamin's house, his principal operations center, or better yet, his clandestine office of human mail. In order to not raise suspicion, the residence was located in one of the most luxurious parts of the city, it was protected by some officials of the main control department who were also in charge issuing illegal identification documents, but valid for travelers like me so that they could move around the country without any problem. In spite that the façade of that residence was very luxurious, the conditions inside were completely chaotic, since a great amount of people from all parts of the world were staying there. All of them with a different religion, culture, and language, but with the same objective: to reach the land of opportunities. Many of them were trapped for several weeks there. Some of them, as a result of their physical appearance were labeled as suspicious and obligated to wait while the guides figured a way to take them out, whilst others simply didn't have the precise amount to continue on their trip. While we made our arrival to the residence, many people, as a result of their physique, could not travel in what could perhaps be seen as a dignified way, but comfortable. They were being packed in the trunks of various cars in order to continue their way. At that moment, the clock marked ten minutes to seven in the morning.

Everyone that was up to date with their stay and transportation tour could enjoy privileges such as: breakfast, dinner, and a modest (but worthy) place to fulfill personal hygiene. The slow payers that did not have enough to cover the stay expenses had to wait for the leftover of the others and also wait to see if a good Samaritan would be moved and would decide to share their small share of food. For personal grooming, they needed to get in line and use the small pool that was in the back patio of the house.

If the north exists, it's because there is a south, and if dominant and dominated countries exist, it's because there are countries that dominate. If our governments were not mediocre or corrupt, no one would have to leave their land leaving everything behind and undertaking a dangerous trip, putting in jeopardy their life with the goal of finding a future that is, in their country, blurred for them and their families. Only words do not allow the feeling of despair that many people have when coming to the land of dreams. It is necessary to live in the flesh in order to know what thousands of clandestine travelers feel, which risked everything to follow a dream, and the hell that they go through is not enough to reach the "*land of liberty and prosperity*". When we reach it, we are catalogued as intruders and usurpers, as if we're a rare species or an epidemic. Many times we are marginalized. If we decide to undertake a risky trip, like this one, it is not because of our own will, but because the majority of us are obligated to leave as a result of this damn corrupt system that we were imposed to.

Fortunately, I had enough money to keep funding my trip. Possessing an identification document that labeled me as a citizen of that country and after receiving several classes from Benjamin to imitate the accent of people from his country, that same afternoon we headed towards the airport to take a flight for about two hours to the capital. I felt bad for the two ladies that came with me to that residence, because they were forced to wait and be packed into the trunks of automobiles, along with many people from other parts of the world. That was the last time that I saw them.

Reviewing all of the recommendations made by Benjamin, I successfully boarded flight two hundred and twenty towards the capital. While I was flying, I began to think of my entire family: my beautiful daughter, everything that I lived through along with Lucas and William, my absurd fights with Charlie over the darn couch, the advice and care of Cenelia, and, although she didn't deserve it, Claudia. It was impossible to not think about her beautiful face, the face of a woman who was partially caused; I missed her more. After all, in the scale of life, the good moments that I lived with her weighed more than the terrible harm she caused me.

When I arrived at the airport of the capital [Mexico City], two immigration agents, that did not buy my story of being a citizen of that country, stopped me. In spite of having worked for a long time acting foolishly, I was unable to make a good voice imitation; the accent of my roots had betrayed me. Then I was taken to an official room of the airport and once there, they did all sorts of interrogations. At that moment thousands of things went through my head. I thought that that would be my last destiny because I would surely return to my place of origin, or, if I were lucky, they would send me to the country to the south. When one of the agents asked me for my identification card that had Benjamin's information, he identified a code in the upper part, on top of the picture; a code that I did not notice when they gave it to me. In spite that the agent could not stop looking at it to prove its authenticity, laughingly he said:

"We know that you're not a citizen of this country, but calm down; you're in good hands. You're a client of Benjamin and we will personally accompany you to the exit"

Thanks to the money I was able to save during the time that I worked with Lucas and William, it was not only helpful to send a good part to my family, but also to buy a clandestine VIP tourism package. Before leaving the airport, Benjamin explained to me what the trip's risks were and gave me three tourist fees that they managed: VIP, superior and regular. In spite of being the most expensive, and having had enough money to pay for it, I did not think twice about it and opted for the VIP because it guaranteed a comfortable trip and safe arrival to my destination, in short time. Another one of the advantages was the stay arrangements, which allowed me to rest in a hotel room that perhaps was not very luxurious, but it was very comfortable, as I waited for the following day to take another flight towards a border town. A city that was well known for being the attraction of hundreds of teenagers that visited from the gigantic neighboring country to the north, due to the great quantity of nocturnal center and the good quality of a miraculous white powder that was sold in its streets; as if it was its infallible morning cup of coffee, they were the main customers.

After well deserved rest, a refreshing warm water shower and receiving the final instruction from Benjamin who called the hotel very early, I was once again leaving on my way to the airport. In spite of feeling very calm for having contracted the VIP package, I couldn't help but entrusting my luck in the powerful universe and the lucky charm that Lucas had given me, which appeared to be working because up to that point my trip had been a success. When I arrived at the airport after fulfilling the routine requirements, I proceeded to follow each one of the directions that Benjamin gave me on the phone. Holding a soda from a local brand, and from a specific flavor, I proceeded to go through security, but before I was able to see two people who were clearly South American like me, who also followed the same instructions verbatim, or rather the same way that I should. Laughing, I said to myself *"surely they also bought the VIP package"*. When I passed through the control area, two of the six officials that were in charge of security before boarding the flight, approached me. They followed the same procedure of the two previous passengers, and they took me to a small room a few steps away from the control area, when one of the agents said a few words as a sort of greeting, which Benjamin had anticipated. I proceeded then to give one of the agents one of the three envelopes that Benjamin had given me before leaving his house; therefore, fulfilling in that way with the indications just like he had asked me to perform.

The agents' gesture showed that the envelope undoubtedly had a payment for being mediators of the clandestine tourist trips. Like people say, *"there's no honesty that a quantity of money cannot buy"*. Those two agents were only another link in the great chain that was involved in the traffic of people. Due to the great profits of that illicit business, from the most common citizen to officials of the highest rank of the controlling departments, they formed part of a giant network of clandestine tourism guides.

Followed by one of the agents that accompanied me to the waiting room, I sat down until it was time to board flight five hundred and thirty, which would take me to the border town. Due to the great weather, the flight was programed to arrive in two and a half hours, but it took exactly an hour and fifty minutes. Thirty minutes after noon, I was already setting foot in that beautiful city, which besides being located in a deserted area its

Due to the immense flow of people that daily circulated through that city, the clandestine guides and the creators of the snow in the city had turned into its base of illegal operations, with no one saying anything. What had before been a warm and hospitable city, had turned into a dangerous and bloody town due to the continuing massacres between the armed groups led by the mafia; groups that fought one another to obtain absolute control of the city. When I arrived at the airport, the first thing I did was give the second of the three envelops to the control agents at the airport, who were already notified of my arrival. This agent, who aside from wishing me luck on the rest of my trip and giving me instructions of the place where I were to stay, gave me a telephone number to get in contact with Beto, who would be my final guide in the most difficult stretch of the tour.

Following the instruction of the agent, I arrived at a small house located twenty minutes from the airport, in the northern most part of the city. Mrs. Camila received me in that place. She also put me in contact with Beto, her nephew. Two hours later after she called him, Beto arrived at his aunt's house in company of two older people coming from two southern states, who had also contracted his services. Before he mentioned a single word, and in order to avoid problems, I took out from my luggage the remaining envelope and I gave it to him; fulfilling verbatim Benjamin's instructions. Beto thanked me for the delivery, and as if he didn't care at least that we knew of the content, he proceeded to open in our presence. Aside from a great sum of cash, the envelope had instruction and coordinates to arrive to the valuable, but extremely harmful and addictive, shipment that needed to be taken to the other side of the border. Through a short chat, Beto explained to us step by step what was going to be the procedure after we left the house.

After that chat, I learned that the VIP package had just expired and it moved to a category below the regular rate. A category that we were all obligated to take for being the only existent one. Beto left the two people that arrived with him and me in his aunt's house and reminded us that we needed to rest and be relaxed for the following day's difficult trip. He went to the street to find more clients to fill the group with give people; a number that was necessary to fulfill the trip's quota. Along with the other two people, I took the place that Mrs. Camila had kindly assigned me. I took advantage of the situation and took a shower, I lay down and was fortunate to sleep a little; all of the events of the trip had assuaged my emotional pain. Later on, Mrs. Camila knocked on my door so I could go out and have dinner. Even though I was in a very comfortable sleep, I got up because it was necessary to eat, because it was not known when there would be a lack of food in such an adventure. At that moment, Beto was already in the house and along with him around the dining room table, two older people, and two more individuals from the Tierra de Fuego [Argentina] which Beto had found. Like me, they looked through all the ways to reach the prominent neighboring country to the worth, which by merely being a few kilometers from that city, it was possible to perceive and feel its grandeur.

The dinner was a pleasant moment because Beto decided to narrate many of the adventures lived through that circle. Those stories gave me morale because I thought of my problems compared to those of other people were more tolerable. Also, I also noticed that I was not the only people whom life had given a strong blow. After a while, and with our mood more relaxed, he invited to take a stroll through the city. At times, I strongly opposed because I did not want to run the risk of being stopped by the authorities, or much worse, fall into the hands of those cruelly and infamously do business with the integrity of people; asking for large quantities of money for their freedom. Additionally, due to my undeniable South American appearance, it was impossible not to be an easy prey for them. But Beto assured me many times that there was nothing to fear; he was well known, but mostly feared in that city because he worked for the highest spheres of criminality, which took care of him and protected him as if he was the president himself. Such type of presentation made me agree to go out, but of course I didn't stop fearing for my security, since I was in a completely strange country and in a city that in spite of being beautiful, its background were not necessarily the best.

By inviting me to take a stroll, Beto was not only inviting me to see his city; he was fulfilling one of the plans of my destiny, because there were still several things for me know, and also to learn. In the wisdom of things my awaited life graduation. While were heading to the center of the city, Beto briefly told me part of his life and the true reason why he decided to enter into the illicit trade of human trafficking.

The terrible economic situation that his country underwent several years ago, coupled with the shortages that deeply affected his family, persuaded his parents to make the hard decision to immigrate to the longed land of opportunity, looking for a better future like the rest of us. At that time, Beto was ten years old and his little sister was eight. Due to the terrible economic crisis that they were going through, they did not have the funds to hire the services of an experienced guide for those types of clandestine trips, so they decided to embark on the adventure themselves. They didn't know that the decision that they made would not take them towards the land of prosperity, but to eternal rest in a nirvana, where his parents and his little sister, Elizabeth, would go.

After having walked lost for several days in the desert, they arrived at a river, which was in the way of prosperity and a better future for all.

Contrary to its name, this appeared to be extremely tranquil, very calm and it even appeared to not to be deep. His parents desire to make to the other side was stronger than their exhaustion and weakness. Then, his dad was convincing Beto to wait ashore while he helped his mother and sister to cross so he could get him after. He carried Elizabeth on his shoulders, took his wife's hand and proceeded to cross the two faced river. Up until a little further from the midpoint, everything was going well. The water was covering them a little over their waists, but a few meters from the shore that would lead them to glory, Beto, from the other shore, became witness of how the ruthless water swallowed them, much to his desperation and impotence for not being able to help them. The worst was having the weight of the last image of his family drowning. I couldn't imagine that, even as he was telling me that I couldn't help but shiver. I couldn't imagine his pain and trauma.

His family was another victim of that tranquil and calm assassin, who had claimed the lives of hundreds of people. As if it conspired or clearly understood the rules of the border patrol, the river impeded at all cost, the entry of wetbacks, as they are called, into its territory. Aside from the large quantities of money that were paid to the clandestine guides for a tour, what was more clandestine were the corpses that lay in the bottom of that silent assassin, or somewhere in the desert. It was the price that some paid for daring to arrive to the land of dreams.

Beto, like every obedient child, had decided to stay in the same place that his dad had left him waiting in. Without being able to do anything to recover his family, sad and defeated, with large quantities of water that came from his eyes, he dedicated himself for days to contribute to the growth of the caudal of the killer of his family. Being alone, lost in the middle of nowhere and without the understanding of why those things happened, at times Beto wanted to give himself to the assailant of his family so that he could also be swallowed and to be able to be with them; however, his fear of death made him desist from his attempts and decided to stay in the shore where his family left him. He prayed to heaven for a miracle to occur and for the assassin to return his family. By being a child that couldn't believe otherwise, that was his only hope. Five days after that tragic event, Beto was found unconscious and dying by the border patrol of his country. They helped him and took him to a health center where they were able to save him. Later, the authorities found Mrs. Camila, his closest relative, and gave her custody.

Beto had been working as a clandestine guide since he was thirteen years old. His experience in it made him knowledgeable of every stretch and centimeter of alternate routes that he used to refer them as *"safe"*. Those routes completely avoided his family's assassin. The reason why he decided to enter that illicit trade was mainly to financially help his Aunt Camila, and secondly to return to the place where his family disappeared, in hopes of finding their remains and give them a worthy burial. But the fundamental reason was to help hundreds of people cross the border in a safe way, and therefore ameliorate the pain, anger and impotence that stayed with him with the death of his parents and sister. He thought that helping other illegals would compensate their death. People that like his family had nothing but their life to gamble.

In the time that he had been working as a guide, no one that had been under his care had disappeared, died or suffered any harm. Beto worried a lot about his clients because he would say that the satisfied client was the

"There are people that are born to be artists; others are athletes, executives, crooks or the equivalent, political and religious leaders. In all, everyone is born with a purpose and this is my calling, I was called for this and I will not go against what is already established. I know that my profession goes against the law and morals, but if it's not me, someone else will do it. Few that do illegal things do it thinking of the good of others, many are only interested in money. The integrity and security of people does not exist for them. I charge my fee, but I make sure that everyone arrives safe and sound to his or her respective destinies, even though this implies risking my own life"

Beto said as he drove his car.

After listening to those words, I knew that I was in good hands. I was conscious that this trip would be very difficult, but with a guide like Beto I was sure that I would arrive safe and sound to my destination. Likewise, I thought about the good luck charm that I had with me, along with the prayers that my mother, my daughter and my entire family pleaded heaven for me. They were having an effect, because from the first day that I left Cenelia's house to the place where I found myself chatting with Beto, gradually things were going to perfection. After all, going out to take that stroll with Beto was the best decision that I made that day, because not only did I get to know my guide better, but also through him I learned to see things from a different perspective. He opened my eyes in respect to the hidden truths, hypocritical faith, fake friendships, the ironies of life and the truths disguised in truth, such as the one that I lived through with the person that I used to call my soul mate. But what I discovered from Beto's testimony, and once more confirmed, that my experience did not compare at all to his.

The stroll through town that Beto took me on was not precisely to see touristy areas, but rather to show me the face of reality. After nearly twenty minutes on the road, we entered an area with poor lighting. In spite of the darkness of the night, the negligence of the area was undeniable. It was a place for all, and also for no one. Forgotten by the experts, by stating the shrewdest lies that vainly promising to work for the neediest people before reaching power; once they obtained what they were looking for, they completely forgot the commitment they made to be elected. That's the way that it happens in the entire world.

The poverty of that area could be seen several meters away. The kids that played on the street recognized Beto's car, became excited, screamed his name and lunged like ants towards the truck. Beto asked me to help him out. He got off his car and from the trunk of the car he proceeded to take out several packages and gave out to each one of the kids, chanting out the name of each of them. To make the delivery easier, Mrs. Camila was in charge assembling the packages and labeled them with the name of each child. Each package had exactly the same: some clothes, a toy and good portion of food; therefore, there was no dispute to obtain the biggest or the best. Aside from giving out the packages, Beto gave a quantity of cash to each of the mother, but warned them that it should be well invested. He, along with his aunt, had been doing that noble humanitarian gesture for some time. Each time that Beto needed to travel, a day before he would visit the area, and two more in different points of the city in order to take them some food. He thought that if something were to happen and he would not come back, those families would have something to eat, at least for a few more days.

"All the money that I have in my pockets, the product of my illegal ventures, it's too much for me. Having it accumulate and spending it on material things that are not spiritually fulfilling is not just. It's for this reason that I decided to share with those that truly need it. Hopefully in this way heaven would turn a blind eye, at least with one of all my sins"

Beto said those words accompanied by a few laughs; he finished delivering the packages.

Once again, satisfied for having fulfilled with his task, invited me to get on his car so we could continue on our trek that still brought things to be learned. After having seen his work I learned with precision what he meant when he said that there were those that did something illegal for the good of others he was one of them, not to say the only one. A mere ten minutes away we arrived at the other side of the coin. The difference to the previous one was that this one had the necessary lightning, and much more, the light of the good life, to be put in a different way. The streets were in perfect condition, with extremely luxurious buildings and security each one of those people, he knew the dark side of the majority. While we were cruising through those luxurious streets, that in contrast to the other neighborhood that was left to oblivion and abandonment; here, there was a scent of expensive perfumes combined with arrogance and superiority. It was then when Beto, with a heated commentary, shed the light on each one of their secrets by saying:

"In places like this is where the real culprits of misery and poverty of thousands people live, such as those of the other neighborhood. In places like these live the corrupt ones that have sunk us to oblivion and who have hypocritically moved laws. According to them, in order to eradicate the addictive garbage that is killing our society. But ironically they are planning the next move on closed doors. In places like these live the hypocrites that promote peace and also fabricate weapons to kill. In places like these live the distinguished ladies of charity, that with their foundation seal they sell to the world the poverty and dignity of others. They obtained juicy donations that are invested in luxurious facades and unending vacations, whilst the poor and wretched don't know if they will eat tomorrow. In places like these live the phonies that make themselves be called kings. In palaces like these live the religious leaders that do business and make millions out of faith, who hypocritically promise to eradicate world hunger and ironically live in a bulletproof palace; spending millions each day in their security, but only to be safe from each other and from the homelessness and filth that their sewers would shine a light on the world. Then he asked me: if I am a delinquent, what are they? The fact that they have a degree or a social and economic status does not make them less of a delinquent than me."

"The mixture of rat and cockroach droppings was slowly mutating into a powerful virus, immune to any invented vaccine: corruption. For being well received and sponsored by politics, it has become the most harmful plague in our society. The world doesn't want hypocrites promoters of peace. The world wants to stop their stupid wars and stop their killings. The world doesn't want the puritan ladies of charity that benefit from the sale of the unhappiness of others. The world wants they work alongside each other, with honesty, for equality. The world doesn't want kings that effortlessly gradually fatten up like pigs in their palaces, whilst millions of poor people sell their souls to the devil eat once a year. The world wants them to auction off their false crown, ask for forgiveness to the universe and to the Jesus, for having usurped his place and make a living form their sweat, like everyone else. The world doesn't want charlatans and false preachers that disguise their hypocrisy, their vagrancy and filth with faith. An image that was self imposed in order to commit crimes; finding refuge behind a doctrine that has been completely altered to their advantage; in spite of this, they're incapable of fulfilling their obligations. Jesus doesn't want his name and his father's to be auctioned off in building that only represent other's own interests. Jesus wants us to continue following his example just as he had established it. Reminding us that religion will not save anyone; what will save us is our vocation to help and serve others with honesty, but especially the true faith towards the invisible. All those corrupt politicians, the hypocrites that promote peace, the ladies of charity that take advantage of others with their false honesty, all the those religious folk that profit over faith, particularly one that everyone knows; but especially all those phonies that call themselves kings, I hope to find them all in hell, in order to spit in their faces and laugh at them." With those words, and laughing hysterically, Beto ended his reflections, as he continued driving his automobile towards the exit of the luxurious neighborhood.

At the beginning, when we arrived, I didn't understand why Beto took me to that place, and I understood much less why he shined a light on the dark side of those people, who I could care in the least about. I thought that the life of those individuals didn't have any effect on mine. But after looking at it from Beto's perspective, I justified that the reason why he took me there. If Beto is from a place different from mine, and in spite of our differences in customs and cultures, he thought like me, surely there were millions of people that thought the same way we did. I meditated.

After we finished doing the things that Beto was accustomed to before each trip, he argued that I couldn't leave his country without trying out what had given them fame worldwide. He invited me to have a drink of the best tequila that was produced in that region. He assured me that it would help me relax for the trip. Without thinking twice, keeping in mind that I needed it, I accepted the shot to verify its fame.

house, Beto thanked me for having accompanied him on that trip, and he reminded me that our trip would begin at eight in the morning the following day. He went to his room to rest and finalize the last details of the trip that awaited us. For my part, I did exactly the same. Thanks to the famous liquor that we drank, I was able to fall asleep a few minutes after I lay down.

Exactly at six in the morning, Mrs. Camila woke up all the people that were traveling with Beto, in order to offer us something to eat and to receive the final instructions. After refueling our energy with a good typical breakfast, we proceeded to leave the house in two groups of three people each. The two older people and Beto left in one group, and the other two people from the Tierra de Fuego and I left in another. Shortly after arriving at the bus terminal, Beto, without giving us details of any explanation in this respect and after buying two large water bottles, suggested, but mainly obligated each of us to buy two more large water bottles and mentioned to stow them with our personal belongings so as to not bring attention to ourselves. Thirty minutes after eight in the morning, we boarded a bus that headed to a town that was close to the Northern border. Following his instruction, we sat in seats that were far away from each other in case one of would be apprehended, preventing our identity from being revealed. It was easier this way for Beto to deal with the authorities.

As the bus was approaching the first checkpoint, nervousness and anxiety was more evident in each one of us. After six hours or so no the road, we arrived at our first checkpoint and the first trial by fire. At the time when the customs and immigration officials stopped the bus we traveled in, three of them got on to inspect it. The other passengers showed much serenity, except those in my group. As far as me, a mountain of nervousness and insecurity overtook me, which alerted one of the dogs of one of the officials who did not think twice of placing handcuffs on me. After several questions of the history and the politics of that country that the official made, with wrong and muted answers on my part, he proceeded to take me off the bus, threatening me with deportation. The other two officials did exactly the same thing with one of the people that came from Tierra de Fuego that traveled in our group. Neither the identification document that Benjamin gave me, or the poor accent imitation of the people from that country could stop the officials from stopping me. Those that were threatening me with keeping me detained assured me that deportation would be my sentence. In contrast to the officials that had stopped me at the capital's airport, who appeared more accessible and friendlier, these appeared excessively arrogant and reluctant to any dialogue.

But at the moment when Beto got off the bus to mediate for us, and the officials found out that we were his clients, the arrogance that they arrested us with suddenly turned into incredible and shocking kindness; they then proceeded to free us from the handcuffs. Evidently, the VIP tourism package that I had purchased was still good, which prevented my apprehension and deportation. Beto joked by telling us to "*dry our pants because everything was under control*", he asked us to board the bus once again before the other passengers would lynch us for having the driver take his time to wait for us.

An hour away from that checkpoint, Beto made an improvised stop and asked the driver to stop the bus so we could get off at that spot. Only kilometers upon kilometers of road, a few mountains afar and the moribund rays of sun that scratched the peak, refusing to die in the sunset, were the only things that were visible in that place. Everything contrasted with the stillness and an absolute silence.

Our guide giving us respective directions of what would be the next step to take, took out one of the bottles of water from his luggage, took a sip, held it and dropped a gush of water on the ground to draw a cross; he warned us to only take sips from that bottle and only when we needed to. Like I, I imagined that at that moment everyone asked themselves the same question: *if we were to drink only one large bottle, why did Beto ask us to carry that quantity of water?* Later, as we were penetrating the desert, I found the answer to that question.

Following the invisible tracks that only his intuition and experience could see and asking us to follow him, Beto marked the beginning of a walk of many kilometers. We crossed mountains and a completely hostile desert that at times threatening to trap us and not let us go. Although the route that Beto knew was very safe to avoid the border patrol, it was filled with natural obstacles that made our mobilization a lot more difficult.

After many hours of an intense walk; following the instruction and coordinates that were in the envelope that I gave Beto, we reached the shipment that days earlier had been sent there so that Beto could be in charge of taking it to the other side of the border. Under the pretext of giving us a few minutes to rest, Beto, extremely happy, justified that with that he would have more money to help more people. He then took out another bottle of water that he had inside his bag and went on to put the brick like packages filled with addiction and perdition in his bag. They were approximately fifteen packages that, through any medium, needed to reach the noses of all the slaves of a narcotic love that they paid anything for feeling a bit of that love running through their veins. Obviously, there was no justification for what Beto was doing, but his vocation for serving and helping others, had led him to do illegal things including risking his life and even own existence. He did it all to help those in some way, but especially through a corrupt system, had abandoned them. I was no one to critique and much less judge what Beto did. The Supreme Judge was the only one that had the power to absolve or condemn each one of his actions.

Once he finished putting away the packets in his bag, he carried the water bottles with his hands and asking us to follow him, he went on to continue with our tour. After that moment, we walked non stop until ten o'clock of the following day. At that time we stopped to find refuge in one of the improvised hideouts that he had, with the goal of keeping us away from the infernal heat of the desert that is common after that time of the day.

Hours before arriving at that hideout, I found the answer to why Beto had made us take that quantity of water. Placing them in strategic places, out of the reach of the sun, and notoriously marking them throughout the way, he put down the water bottles as he explained that it was to save the life of the people that constantly would get lost in that part of the desert; that is, whether they decided to take the trip on their own or because they were the victims of unscrupulous guides who after obtaining their money left them on their own in the middle of the desert. With that noble gesture he gave us a lesson of solidarity to all, making us see that with a little effort, and sharing a minimal part of what we have, we can make a big difference.

After staying there for many hours in that hideout, we took advantage of the arrival of the night, with more bearable climate, and we followed our guide beginning what would be the last and most decisive walk. As we reached the invisible line that separated the North from the South, the desire to have everything end soon was more ostensible in each one of us. The exhaustion and physical wear, which were beginning to claim its first victims; age, the long and intense hours of walking, coupled with a lack food, made Rodolfo, one of the older people that came with us, faint, which delayed our trip for nearly two hours. As we waited and helped him recover, we took advantage of the moment by taking a break and a few sips of water from the only water bottle that Beto left for us. Once Rodolfo recovered, we continued on our way, but we didn't take our eyes off him for a single moment. We were only three or so hours away from completing our objective and we didn't want for any reason in the world to be caught by the border officials that guarded that side of the border.

Evidently, Beto's senses became more acute with each trip he took; only he could see and hear at a great distance the border police vehicles that as a haunter looking for a prey, moved silently from one side to the other. A few kilometers away from our objective and with the first rays of light that shined from the horizon, the presence of the vehicles of the border patrol were more visible for all of us, and as we advanced we felt them closer each time. At times we thought that we would be stopped since Beto was taking us directly towards them. We walked in one direction, but it was a strategy of his to distract them; playing cat and mouse, where the mouse, due to his guile and ingenuity, had a great advantage over the giant feline.

It was a trick that was very well elaborated in this way: at a distance considerably far from the checkpoints, and much before they noticed our presence, Beto was apart from us, making the officials only notice him; forcing them to believe that he was lost or that he was the only one trying to cross the border. While the officials placed all their attention on him, we were reaching the other side of the border calmly, crossing almost in front of their noses. He left us at the entrance of a secret subterranean passage, or more of a drain of about three to four kilometers in length, which connected directly with the other side of the border. A few minutes from exiting this tunnel, laughing out loud, Beto caught up to us as he mocked the officials. We still had a stretch more to go, but the excitement began to rein in each one of us because the most complicated we had already passed, and we were a few minutes from reaching victory.

California, USA]. At the same time, this made us feel as if everything was worth the effort. At that moment, several feelings filled with happiness and excitement took over not only my face, but also the others' as well. The excitement was such that, any person that has accomplished a dream or a goal would understand what I'm talking about. Setting foot on prosperous soil, filled with opportunities for a better future for my family and me.

As it is said, every cloud has a silver lining after all. Starting a movement against the political slag of my country not only allowed me to reach the Great Land of Opportunities, but also to learn great things and meet unique people that life put in my path throughout my trip. The universe, as an infinite magician, fulfilled one of the wishes that I had since I was a child. The unattainable images that I only saw through a television screen, at that moment, I could feel and even touch.

At the time that we arrived at the home of one of the people that worked with Beto in that side of the border, he had confirmed that the trip had ended with success and there was nothing to worry about, happiness was extremely indescribable in each one of us, even Beto appeared very happy. In the Anglo territory, although the risks were inevitable, it was much easier move from one state to the other; that same afternoon, everyone took different routes to different states of the nation, where their relatives and friends awaited them. The people from the Tierra de Fuego headed towards the Sun Capital, the other older folks left to the Windy City and I headed towards the Big Apple, where my friends were waiting for me.

For his part, Beto stayed to rest and spend the night in the house of one of his colleagues as he waited for the person in charge of spreading snow in that city to come and pick up the mail he needed to deliver. In a small chat I had with Beto in his colleague's house, I asked him why he didn't work in this country, he laughed at my comment and answered that if he worked day and night, he would be able to make the kind of money he does in every trip. Moreover, he does more and provides more help by being on the other side. Beto was very committed to his social cause; the death of his family had marked him forever. So much so that he made the promise that he would be a good guide for the people to cross the border in a safe way, in order to avoid their loss of life by taking dangerous routes, as it happened to his parents and sister by not counting with the help of an experienced guide.

After every trip, Beto would return to visit the place where his family lay in order to take them flowers and thank them. He felt as if they were the true guides that showed him the way where he should take his tourists. His vocation to help and serve the others surpassed limits; in addition to helping people from poor neighborhoods of the city, he would always bring two people with him, in order to help them cross the border at absolutely no charge. They of course needed to be people of scarce resources; according to him, this was his secret for good luck so that his trip would be successful. In exchange, he would also ask them to extend prayers to heaven pleading for him. The older folks that traveled with us were the fortunate ones to have travelled free.

Independently from the illicit things that Beto did, this did not cancel out merits for being a good human being. Along with Cenelia, Lucas and William, Beto became part of the list of special friends. Until this day we continue talking and every time that he comes with a group of tourists he tends to call me to chat. Evidently, the prayers of all the people he helped along with his good actions, which weighed more than the illegal things that he did, conspired for the universe to turn a blind over his bad actions.

Due to the distance from coast to coast that I had to travel, it took me approximately three days to reach my final destination and since then, I have been in this incredible city, along with all that fight day to day, contributing with the growth of this great nation, but also taking a bit of its wealth to help my family."

"How long have you lived in this city?"

My friend asked once he finished telling me his interesting trip.

"In contrast with you, I have relatively a short time living in this city." I answered, making the following question:

"In all the time that you have been living in this country, have you traveled to visit your family?"

"Unfortunately, I haven't been able to do it since I don't have a visa to travel, but very soon I will be a universal citizen and will be able to travel to visit them as many times as I want. Best of all, I will be able to travel the world without the need to carry documentation or a visa. I know that

The statement that he made at the end appeared to be so bizarre that they left me very confused and even with a big of panic because I didn't know what he meant by this.

"By the way, the invitation for breakfast that Mathew extended to you, why don't we leave it for the tomorrow. He will be very happy to see you, and we could use the time to chat and take a stroll through the city"

My friend concluded before saying goodbye that Wednesday morning. The crossing story that my strange friend had told me was very extensive and it practically took me all night to transfer it to my computer. At the time when I turned it off and recuperated the notion of time, the clock dialed six twenty in the morning of a new day: Thursday.

Chapter 4

Thursday,
A Pending Breakfast,
An Important Lesson to Learn

In spite of having absolutely not slept, I felt very relaxed and calm. That day was going to be completely different for me, not only because I had a pending invitation for breakfast, but also because I was going to fulfill the deal I had made the day before, daring to do something that I had never done; so, I did it. Although, this implied that I would receive the scolding from my boss for the accumulated work that needed to be done in advance.

In contrast to other days that I worked ahead of schedule, that morning I completely lost track of time and did my things with the most tranquility. After a comforting shower that helped be stay lucid, and adding to it a greater dose of caffeine, as always I sat down to watch the news to delight myself with my platonic love, my unattainable dream of every morning whilst in the middle weather forecast. I could've forgotten to do anything, even eating, but I couldn't leave the house without seeing her. Those minutes that our encounter lasted were the most special for me, perhaps they were work, but those moments were a window to the imagination for me. Joking with myself on various occasions, I told myself:

"I'm sure that next to such beauty I would look handsome."

Following with rigor the tip that my platonic love recommended: to leave house well covered up, since the temperatures once again had dropped below the freezing point, and fulfilling the promise I made myself, I drew a smile on my face and left my house towards the subway station. Aside from the terrible cold that once again visited us, which the crude winter that was predicted remained still, the city was relatively calm.

Before arriving to the metro station, remembering that I had pending invitation for breakfast, we passed through a cafeteria that was a few blocks from the metro station in order to buy what Mathew suggested the day that he made the invitation. Supplying myself with enough coffee and donuts, I continued my way towards the metro station. Due to few people that were in the station, the visibility in it was very clear. Just like other days, my friend was already inside the station, but this time, he was standing several meters from the spot where I had found him three days earlier; ready to board the first train wagons; it was something that I didn't care in the least, I had thought of doing the same.

"I see that you kept your word of coming with us to breakfast." Said my friend after greeting me.

"My word is worth more than any signed document, that's why I wouldn't have missed this commitment."

I answered with a smile.

"Mathew was very thankful for your greeting and surely he'll be happy to see you."

He said again.

"Mathew seems to be an excellent person, I always see him happy." I said, totally convinced.

"He's an exceptional person, when you get to know him better you will appreciate him more. He has also been one of my great tutors towards my brilliant graduation from life. When you get to know him better, you will know what I'm talking about, I hope that you have some spare time today because after breakfast, Mathew and I want to show you a few things."

He answered winking.

"Although it might imply being scolded or even being fired by my boss, today I have decided to omit the order of Ms. routine; I took the day off so I have the enough time."

I answered laughing.

"Don't worry, just like Mathew and I, you will no longer be a slave of time."

My friend answered, leaving me confused with that commentary, but that time I was willing to stay with the incertitude of knowing what he meant with those words. Looking for clear answer, I asked:

"Why do you say that?"

But at the precise moment when he was getting ready to give me an answer, the train appeared from out of nowhere in the station, leaving the answer that I wanted lost in the limbo.

Breaking the habit that I had of always boarding the train in the same spot, just like the day before, that morning I boarded the train in one of its first wagons, and my friend did exactly the same. When we saw that the train was somewhat empty and with available seats, we sat near the heater so it would warm us up. In contrast to other days when I had an established destiny every time I boarded the metro; that morning I got on without the least idea of where I was going, the only thing I knew was that I had an invitation to have breakfast and that we would later take a stroll through the city; that's all I knew.

With the smile I drew on my face after having seen my platonic love before leaving my house, fulfilling the promise that no one was going to erase it, I freed my courtesy once more and began to greet all the people that would not stop looking at me surprised. I wished them a good day and ignored them.

"I see that you're beginning to positively accept the unexpected situations in life; this is good because by complaining or being bitter, the only this you're doing is accelerating aging. Ultimately, we are here to be happy, the universe gave us this wonderful world to enjoy its infinite beauty regardless of circumstances."

Said my friend, when he saw the action that I began to adopt.

"You are right, that's why I promised that I would smile at least twice a day."

I answered with a spontaneous smile.

Between laughs, we didn't notice that the train was arriving at the him two small plastic bags. He came in and sat, as usual, in front of us. I expected to see the other passengers run away towards other wagons to escape the unmistakable scent of musk, which they always did. I didn't know what happened that morning, but curiously no one got up; moreover, absolutely no one acknowledged his presence. The laughter that I waited to have when the other passengers escaped to avoid being contaminated by his aroma was trapped in my throat because they were apathetic to his presence. *Too bad*! I thought. Because the desire to laugh was really my only ironic and diplomatic way to mock people and get back at them for the indolence they used to judge me with.

I thought that he would stretch his hand to greet me, but it was not the case. He simply greeted me with amiability, leaving me with my arm extended and I thought that it was impolite in his part. On top of that, I began to hear several laughs and murmurs between the passengers. Once again were those accusing stares, which would say: *"that man is either crazy or high"*. I knew that they could see me, but not my other two friends, and like the other times I lost a hold of myself, but this time for other reasons. I couldn't understand why, I also couldn't perceive the scent of months without a shower that Mathew would have. It was then when I began to throw several questions trying to find an answer to Mathew's sudden change. Amongst the several questions that I made myself were: *"why didn't Mathew bring all his belongings? Why don't people notice his presence?"* and, *"why didn't he stretch his hand to greet me like he did last time?"* I came up with the conclusion to all those questions and deduced that it had to do with the breakfast invitation; he simply wanted to look good and for that reason he allowed water to perform a miracle and left without his junk to move about tranquil because we were going to take a stroll that was planned with anticipation. But what I couldn't explain was why he didn't stretch my hand like he always did. The day that I had reserved to relax and free myself from the stress of the routine appeared not to have a good start.

"What's going on Jeremy, you appear a bit tense. Calm down, relax that life is meant to smile and be happy. Towards the unexpected circumstances of life, it is important to always adopt a positive attitude."

Said my friend, as Mathew agreed by his nodding his head.

"You're right, but wouldn't you think the same if you had all those strange smiles on you, condemning you as if you were insane."

I answered with sort of a bad mood.

"Until they find themselves in the same situation as you, they will never understand what's going on, or what happens around us. Remember that life is a circle, they are now your accusers, but tomorrow or the day after, those roles will invert and you will be in their place, and them, in yours. There, I'm sure you will think exactly the same as them, so try to relax, free yourself from biases and you will see that everything will get better for you."

Answered Mathew, giving me some tranquility.

Such wise words would make anyone unable to believe that someone like Mathew that appeared homeless, could calm a man down; who in contrast to him, he was in better conditions. But these are the ironies of life. In spite that I had taken that metro line for a long time, I only knew the way from my house to work and vice versa. The rest of the route and the metro station were a world completely unbeknownst to me. It was the first time that I dared to leave the space that I had confined to dare to destabilize the order of my routine. As the train left my world and I opened my space and mind to the other, I felt like a stranger, unknown to in my own house. I found it funny that I appeared like a tourist lost in a great city. On the hand I felt like a prisoner that just escaped his cell.

"I see that you bought enough donuts to satiate the hunger of an entire regiment, if it weren't because my body was purified and lost the sensibility in my palate, I assure you that I would devour them at this instant. But we have to wait to arrive at the place that we chose to have breakfast in. By the way, it's a surprise, but I'm sure that you will like it. There will be neither coffee nor donuts that will survive the ferocious hunger of my other guests that are piggish like me."

Said Mathew laughing out loud in the middle of the chat.

Again, Mathew confused with his words because he gave the impression that he was speaking in code. The only one that appeared to understand him with exactitude was my friend. He corroborated with each one of his taste buds, I thought that it was caused for having eaten something hot. But it appeared to be very weird, because that means he would've had to eat a hot coal for that. And when he talked about the rest of the guests, I was perplexed because I didn't know where I was going, and because I was convinced that the three of us would share the first meal of the day.

"By the way Jeremy, thanks for your greeting, it's good to know that friends remember."

Mathew told me showing me a face of happiness that at times I didn't know where all that joy came from. I was not used to that because I am generally sparing and he exceeded the limits of happiness.

"You don't have to thank me, it was nothing; I only hope that you also remember me when you don't see me."

I told him as I laughed a little.

"Be sure of that, not only will I remember that I will always remember you in my prayers."

Mathew answered, transmitting an overdose of good energy.

"I thank you infinitely for having the absurd idea of wanting to beat time and especially being carried away by my ego. Thinking of it as unnecessary, it has been a long time since I stopped elevating my prayers to heaven."

I answered a bit embarrassed.

"Don't worry that you're not the only one. The routine and idea of always wanting to beat time; thinking that we are eternal has turned us into machines that only think in producing and making money. In spite that the day is twenty four hours long, we are incapable of taking a second to thank our maker for being alive and enjoy the infinite beauty of the world. After all, our forgetfulness for the all powerful universe is not much, in His wisdom, He is very kind and does not recent us. If you once again take up the habit of praying to heaven and do it from the heart, you will see that He will let go of the time that you had forgotten Him, filling you with infinite peace, but specially with thousands of blessings. It will fill you with infinite interior peace, but also with thousands of blessings. So Jeremy, it is better now than never."

With those words Mathew made me realize that there's no excuse to take a few minutes from all the time the universe gives us, to be thankful for all we are and for all we have. As the conversation advanced and with each word that Mathew mentioned, he was giving me basic lessons of spiritual growth. After a transfer we made at the Union Square station to another line that would take us the bottom most part of lower Manhattan, Mathew and my friend told me that there was something that he wanted to show me.

Before going to breakfast, they took me to one of the viewpoints that was located in the west part of the Hudson River. It was the first time that I set foot in that spectacular place, with such an incredible view. "*The things that one misses out on by not taking the time to see them*", I thought as I admired such wonder. I also reproached myself for having set limitations that only allowed me to see the space that I had created for myself; knowing that there was a infinity of things to see and discover in this wonderful limitless world.

Overpassing the security restrictions imposed by the authorities, Mathew and my friend stood on one of the railings over a contention barrier that separated the waters from the Hudson from land. They then opened their arms and allowed for the freezing breeze to caress their faces. Like two kids that for the first time had gone out to an amusement park, they began to yell deafening screams of joy, whose loudness did not seem to bother other people at all; people who were mostly tourists and tried to immortalize the incredible view of that place with a photographic image.

"Hopefully they don't think we're crazy; it's only a practical way to liberate our tensions, making us feel as if we are owners of this wonder that nature gives to us. Sometimes we do it here; sometimes we do it from one of the hundreds of skyscrapers of this or any other city; sometimes from the highest point of the structure of a bridge, and from wherever we want, because we are free and we enjoy the privileges of being universal citizens. Perhaps you don't understand what we're talking about, but you will soon know; that moment comes to all of us."

My friend told me, as Mathew dared me to scream like them.

The words that he had just told me left in shock for a few seconds. It was surely a joke, because only a bird can only perch in such high places, I thought a bit confused. But at the sight of such unleashed adrenaline only listen to myself, since I didn't want to get the attention of the other people. Mathew and my friend made fun of me and told me that even the flight of a fly was louder than my screams. Then my friend showed me what needed to be done and dared me to do it just like it or even louder than them. Following his lead, and with my legs shaking like gelatin, I slowly leaned on one of the railings, opened my arms with apprehension, and when I had them completely open I discovered that freezing breeze on my face and began to scream again and again; each time it was louder, I imagined that I was flying.

"That's the attitude: just be free, be yourself and don't let others get in the way of what you want to do. Demonstrate that you feel good and are happy doing it. I assure you that one or two people will follow your example and do exactly the same. Feel like a guide, but mostly be secure of yourself."

Mathew told me insistently as he turned his head to fill his lungs and continue screaming.

In contrast to the deafening screams of Mathew and my friend that did not appear to reach the eardrums of the other people that were in that spot; curiously, as soon as I began to scream, various people immediately turned towards me.

"It is a simple and practical way to release stress and lower tension; it's a good therapy that has given me good results. You should try it."

I told everyone, following Mathew's advice. And I went on to catch my breath in order to continue screaming and releasing my stress.

It was then when aside from listening to Mathew's screams, my friend's and mine, I began to hear the screams of a pair of teenagers that decided to join the choir. Then, what had started as a three person choir, turned into an avalanche of screams. Mathew was right, it was only necessary for someone to take the first step. He explained that it was for a good cause, in order for the rest to do exactly the same. That's expected from the guides and leaders: to be a valid and honest example to follow.

After liberating the stress and lower tension with that scream therapy, we went to one of the coin operated binoculars, which allowed us to look in detail at the beautiful scenery, making more visible what our eyes do not see.

Mathew, pointing toward the solitary lady, symbol of liberty, invited me to see her. And there was that beautiful lady that, in spite of living in the same city as her, I had never dared to visit her. Shamefully, I had only seen her in posters, photographs, and movies or in replicas sold in souvenir shops.

"What do you see?" Mathew asked.

"I see the imposing figure of the lady, symbol of liberty."

I answered, astounded by the spectacular images that filtered through my eyes.

"Your look of amazement makes me think that this is the first that you've seen her in person, I'm I wrong?"

Mathew asked me again.

"Although you might not believe it, this is the first time that I have seen this place and it's the first time I've seen her in person."

I answered excited at the sight of such marvel.

"The universe is so perfect that it put us in this world free, in order to live in harmony and to enjoy all of its grandeur, and on simple things like admiring that image."

Mathew finished saying that.

He was right. By not having the guts to go outside of my own limits, I was depriving myself and missing out on enjoying all the great things of this world; things that do not necessarily require being a millionaire to live unforgettable moments. A simple visit to the park, perhaps a beach, a picnic or simply a walk through the city, it's more than enough to make us feel alive. After having vented out a bit my freedom and having learned about the impact and importance of simple things, the three of us went on to enjoy a promising breakfast with the rest of the guests. Mathew suggested accelerate the pace because they were probably impatiently waiting for our arrival. We then headed east, directly under the Brooklyn bridge, where we would have our breakfast and where the rest of Mathew's and my friend's guests were waiting.

Several shopping carts parked under the bridge, similar to the one Mathew had on the day I met him; filled with cardboards, plastic bags and all sorts of weird objects. There was also an improvised bonfire inside a large metal trashcan, in order to avoid the spreading of the fire to other parts.

same social status as Mathew. One by one he introduced them to us, and they all received us with joy. The human warmth of those people, more than the bonfire, helped to greatly minimize the freezing cold of that morning.

Once he finished introducing me to his friends, Mathew asked permission to take the donut box and, along with my friend, they began to serve the other five people who aside from us, were also in that place. As we sat there looking at each other and meeting one another, one of them joked about having the donuts with a cube of coffee that had literally been frozen by the intense cold. Naturally we had to warm it up, and then one of them took out a small metal pot and placed it over the fire. When we started to eat, I was surprised because Mathew and my friend served the coffee and the donuts in equal portion for all, except for them, especially Mathew who was the most enthusiastic with that breakfast. So I asked then why they didn't have breakfast if there was enough for them.

"Why you, but mostly why do they need to eat more than us, the food that we need is provided directly by the universe to the spirit."

Mathew answered, leaving me more confused because as much as I tried I couldn't understand what he meant by those words.

"Calm down, you should've get frustrated thinking about what we're trying to say, because you will very soon know what we are talking about. So, relax and enjoy your breakfast."

My friend said, trying to calm me down.

Mathew and my friend, after giving thanks, first to heaven for that special moment that was given to us, and then to me for having bought the coffee and donuts that helped to partially satiate the hunger of those people, began to sing and tell jokes. They tried to animate the get together.

The rest of Mathew's and my friend's guests also thanked me for the good food that I brought. They asked me again to come, and with their good sense of humor, one of them warned that only in the condition of taking an extra order of coffee and donuts to save for later.

Of course, I laughed because it was not a problem for me to share with them and also because in spite of them poor people, I had never felt like I had such a good breakfast under a bridge.

"The one you need to thank is Mathew, and yes, of course I'll be back. For me it will be a great please to come back to visit you. And don't worry, I'll make sure not only bring one, but two orders of donuts to devour."

I also responded laughing.

"The universe is so generous and kind that it never forgets about us. Today it was you, perhaps tomorrow it'll be someone else, but it always sends us someone to feed us. Lives' circumstances made us forgettable and marginalized by society, but to the universe we are equal like everyone else. Under all of society's and ours' poverty there exists the same chemical powder component with which we were all created."

Responded one of Mathew's guests, leaving me speechless and unable to know what to say.

When I heard those words, I had a knot in my throat and my heart wanted to leave my chest, but even I felt part of that marginalizing society. Before meeting Mathew, on my way I always found people like them I was never capable of helping them. Feeling absurdly important and superior to them, I ignored them completely, even though they only wanted me to return the greeting that they kindly gave me. By hearing those words I didn't feel worthy to be amongst those people. I even felt extremely ashamed of myself, because one of those people reminded me of my father, who, by various circumstances, distanced himself from us when I was a kid and I randomly found him after several years in the same situation as them. In spite of having seen him alone, hurt and needy, I was not capable of doing anything to help him. My prejudices allowed me to give him a miserable and cold hug, and I left, leaving him abandoned to his luck. It's something that I will never forgive myself forever. Now that it's too late, I want to mend things, but it's useless because he's no longer here. *I only hope that from his eternal rest, one day he could forgive me*", I thought in silence as I avoided tears from falling.

The wit and jokes from Mathew and my friend prevented the breakfast from falling into melancholy and pain as a result of bad thoughts, which made us all show off our comedian skills that turned the gathering into laughs upon laughs. Never in my life had I laughed as much as I did that morning, so much so that I was in agreement with those that say that laugher is best medicine for the soul; therefore, it helps keep the spirit young. That breakfast morning, I felt like a twelve year old kid again. I always

At around two in the afternoon, each one taking their belongings and leaving the place clean and neat so that the authorities would not have complaints of them and would allow them to keep using the spot; they thanked us for everything and each one went their own way. They needed to arrive on time to find a space in one of the many homes and shelters that the city offered as protection for the winter, which tends to be more intense at nightfall. Us, on the other hand, took the metro towards Brooklyn. My friends decided to take me to see the foundation that Mathew assisted, either to spend the night or to simply receive a plate of food. As I was in the metro I asked myself, why did Mathew and my friend decide to take me to that place, but when I arrived I found my answer.

When we arrived, I saw the magnitude of that foundation or mainly its structure; I was left surprised. Contrary to what I had imagined, this was a building that was very large and modern, very well equipped, but only for housing people without a home, but also for tending to medical emergencies. When we entered that establishment, Mathew and my friend inexplicably rushed ahead of me, leaving me the responsibility of justifying to the reception why we were there.

"The reason why I'm here is because I would like to see the facilities of this place and see if there is a way that I can contribute."

I told one of the people at the reception a bit embarrassed after I greeted her.

She kindly returned the greeting, gave me a welcome as she assigned a person to be my guide.

"It's not necessary; I have my own guide."

I told her as I pointed at Mathew who was with my friend, standing next to a voluntary medic that lent his services to that place.

Then, the receptionist thanked me for my visit and allowed me access without any objection.

Once inside, Mathew began to show me each one of the places in the building, and as if it was his house, with much authority he showed me each one of the different sections, distributed in each one of the eight floors that made up that building. He knew each corner of that place.

"Surely he's asking himself how this place is sustained, *right?* But before you come to your own conclusions, let me answer. The majority of the people that you see working here are volunteers; wonderful people that in exchange for nothing, they dedicate their time to help and serve the needy. A great part of private donations, and another percentage of funds given by the city for social help is what keeps this place running and working correctly."

Mathew explained as he took me to the shelters that occupied a great majority of the plant.

Hundreds of people, mostly homeless, and other that for other circumstances didn't have a place to live, occupied the shelter. In their faces a crude reality of life was drawn, that in spite of being in a first world country, they had fallen in the misfortune of abandonment or economic scarcity.

"If in a nation that is said to be extremely rich and powerful, there still exists poverty, with more reason it is present in our countries. Corruption and governmental mediocrity have made us fall not only in poverty, but misery and the indifference to accept it all."

I said as we left that place and headed towards another part of the building.

"Regrettably, corruption and the ambition to obtain everything easily has taken several nations towards poverty, with thousands of people going through hunger and suffering, while the culprits of those atrocities live in crystal palaces…perhaps they are immune to their own invented convenient justice, but when the moment comes, in the Celestial Court in front of the Supreme Judge, all their money will not prevent the deserved sentence that the universe will impose on them."

Mathew answered adding:

"*'To the Caesar what is Caesar's and his clowns to the circus'*, we will continue with ours, since the universe will take care of them."

"You're right; it's not worth to ruin the moment by talking about those rodents."

I told them laughing as we headed towards the third floor, assigned to the unit of intensive care and terminal illnesses.

After visiting some patients from intensive care, which in spite of their gravity showed signs of improvements, we went to visit the patients with terminal illnesses that held on until the last second of their lives. At that loveless by his family and friends, he decided to give up in our presence. He allowed the evil cancer to end his life.

"Moving scenes like that is the everyday bread of this place. But thanks to the love and care of the people that work here, the life of many patients is at least lengthened one more day. Many of them show in their faces the cruel abandonment of their families. Some of them, after having spent many years selling their solitude and fighting alone against their disease, part from this world in a cold and empty bed, without anyone to shed a single tear for their passing. We know that we're part of the universe, but getting free will we allowed our hearts to get deformed in perversities capable of giving our backs to our loved ones. When they were alive, we never show them how valuable they are or how much we love them; after several years of abandonment, they hypocritically come to cry to a cold soulless body. They know that after death, their faked lament is worthless."

Very sad and with tears in his eyes, Mathew expressed his feelings in front of the body of that man. It was the first time that I saw Mathew sad, and with good reason; scenes like that pierce the deepest part of our soul.

This was the answer to the code words of my new friends. Anchored in the opposite face of what I was accustomed to see. Then, not only did I justify the reason of why they took me there, but also I understood that I needed those crude and real examples to value what I have; appreciating each second the wonderful gift that it is to live, and demonstrating more affection to the people that I love who are alive, because it doesn't make sense after death.

After that harsh lesson, we arrived at the fifth floor. There, we visited the loyal lover to a love that in spite of being white, it turns your life completely black. Mortal and toxic, a love that had them addicted to their enchantment; a love for all and no one; a love that is extremely unfaithful and destructive; a love that gives you wings and takes you to the precipice. It's a love perverted and selfish, which loves you if you pay for its favors. The majority of the people that were in that place were teenagers that wanted to experiment the sensation of that love running through their veins. They didn't know that they would end up being slaves of a soulless love, without flesh and feelings, which slowly was taking them to the abyss.

Mathew and my friend took a seat in one of the benches of the hallway. I on the other hand, contemplated everything I had just seen and then wanted to chat with those people, who were mostly younger determined to be free at once from that false passing love. After befriending and talking for a long while with them, I assured them that I would return to visit; I said goodbye and walked with my friends towards a small room designated for group therapies, where each person exposed their own testimonies, experiences and life events with their narcotic love. When I came in, I saw in its walls something that I liked very much; it was several verses that were written between those addicted people as part of their therapy, in order to demonstrate that they were capable of liberating themselves from what destroyed them most.

"Our body is the temple of the universe; we must keep it clean and free from contamination. Chemical substances not only harm and contaminate our organism, but also debilitate our spirit."

Mathew said at the moment when I approached them to continue what would be our last visit in the seventh floor.

"Sometimes, the weakness from our flesh is stronger that our own reason and we end up foolishly harming ourselves needlessly; but thanks to places like these and to our reasonableness, addictions could only be a bad moment. Perhaps we will not be able to completely decontaminate our bodies, but we are able to stop it from ending our lives in the worst possible way."

Answered my friend, corroborating with Mathew's words.

When we arrived at the seventh floor, we entered the section of suicidal patients who were treated carefully by the medical personnel in order avoid any type of mishap with their patients. It was a very sad picture: people walking from one place to the other, many of them talking and gesturing with their imaginary friend; other, due to their grave mental state, accompanied only by their loneliness, were isolated in four cotton walls, cushioning their self abuse. It was the tragic scene that could be seen in that place. I don't know if it was either by change, or because my friends already knew what was going to happen. They deliberately took me to that place so that I could participate in the surprise that life what saving for me that day.

fell apart and automatically my eyes created a great tempest. I couldn't believe who I was looking at: it was one of my best friends that came with me to this country; like me, he also came trying to accomplish his dreams. I knew him from childhood and curiously a long time had passed since I heard from him. Ironically I found him in that situation and in that melancholic place. When he looked up, I thought he would recognize me, but it was not the case; his mind wandered into limbo, condemned to his body to live like a zombie. At that moment I felt like a miserable person, because I did not give him any attention when he was calling to tell me of his solitude and depression. He was looking to chat with someone and asking me to go visit him. Carried by my damn selfishness, I always invented excuses not to do it.

If life, Mathew, and my friend were trying to give me a lesson, that day they were able to do so by putting in front of me that zombie like image of my best friend, which was in part caused by my stupid selfishness. With the impotence of not being able to do anything for him to recover consciousness, or revert back in time, preventing his sadness by the abandonment he felt, I left carrying with me his memories and his image that screamed how selfish I was.

"That's the essence of humankind; we never value or take advantage of what we have at that moment and when we lost it, we lament and scold ourselves over whether what would've happened if we had done something at the appropriate time. Regret perhaps helps, but does not remedy at all the situation. Don't take it personal; I'm talking about the entire world."

Mathew told me, as he touched my shoulder as we headed towards the elevators to leave that building.

If those words mentioned by Mathew were aimed at me, I felt it was well deserved because even thought I felt like an exemplary being, I saw that it's not enough with just being respectful, perhaps kind and somewhat generous. With the visit to that place, the universe, Mathew and my friend reminded me of thousands of things that I needed to learn in order to become the laudable man I wanted to be.

Shortly before we reached the exit of the building, Mathew and my friend once again walked a few meters ahead of me, exiting first from the building, leaving me behind. The reason they did this, coming up with my own conclusions, I was able to know two days later. At the moment that I was going to cross the door towards the exit, the same person at the reception who greeted me, made me wait to ask a few questions.

"The doctor that you told me would be your guide never went with you. Moreover, he said he didn't know you. I wonder then, who was the person that accompanied you to tour the facilities of this place."

She asked me smiling.

"When I pointed at the person that would be my guide, I was not referring to the medic, but some friends that were standing next to him. Actually, they just left a few seconds ago."

I answered, also smiling.

"Your friends must be invisible or ghosts because I didn't see them come in with you, or much less leave at any moment."

She responded, adding a few laughs to her enchanting smile.

"Maybe you didn't get to see them, but I assure you that they left through that door."

I said, showing confidence in one of my words.

Thanking me for the visit, and making a deal with me so that the next that I visit that place she would be my guide and so that, according to her, I would stop inventing absurd stories. She then let me leave that place without any objections. Responding to her kindness and closing the deal with a strong handshake, I left that place very moved and shocked by all that I experienced inside.

On top of all the surprises that I had that day, a snow stormed accompanied by the darkness of the night surprised me when I left the building, which made mobilization and visibility difficult. Since the winter schedule made days relatively short during that time of the year, it was four thirty at that moment and it was completely dark outside. Guided by the sound of their voices that mentioned my name when they called me, I was able to make out Mathew and my friend who were refuged under the small roof of a bus stop across the street.

"These are great things that the universe gives to us; what a great way to end the day."

Voiced Mathew as he threw a snowball over me.

My friend screamed, as he also threw another snowball at me, which created a great disadvantage of two versus one.

Responding to their reception, I threw a snowball to each one and walked closer to them to start a heated free for all bombardment, with the white and harmless ammunition that fell from the sky. After an intense war where no one wanted to give up, Mathew said: *"true and sincere friendship should be remembered forever"*, he proposed a truce to build snowmen that would represent each one of us. Also, we needed to dress them with pieces of our clothing; Mathew dressed his snowman with his scarf, my friend dressed his with his coat, making him be only in his shirt, which did not seem to bother him at all. I on the other hand, dressed mine with one of my favorite hats that I had one that day and that also had a special meaning for me. After winding back for a long time to our childhood, playing war and soldiers like kids in the middle of the snow, and making those effigies that represented each one of us; we left to take the metro and return home, leaving our noble doubles in the bus stop, so that everyone could appreciate our talent as sculptors.

Getting out of my own limits not only helped me to see another part of the city that I lived in, but also to learn extremely valuable things. On our way back home, I thought about everything that happened that day, and that a simple invitation for breakfast turned into a day filled with surprises that made me see how wrong I was in respect to the exemplary person I thought I was. Mathew and my friend turned into my masters; they showed me that either with little or nothing one could be happy, but especially sharing and giving ones best without waiting to receive something in return.

"Jeremy, we will not tell you goodbye, because very soon we will see you, but this time it will be in a very different place; go rest, relax and thanks for having accepted our invitation; it was an spectacular day."

Mathew and my friend told me as they said goodbye to me, while they were getting off at the Union Square station to board another line that would take towards the Bronx.

"It was a very special day. It was worth missing work, and if I have to hear the scolding from my boss, I will gladly do it because what I discovered and learned doesn't compare to the money that I could've made."

I answered laughing as I said goodbye to them.

Thinking about all the things that I happened that day, amongst them the strange and mysterious words that Mathew and my friend mentioned at time, but specially the words that they said at the time when we said goodbye. In all, from station where I said goodbye to them, until my arrival home, the journey seemed a little short. In a little over thirty minutes I was at the store of my friend Hassan, like I had every day.

"The great good luck blows that we gave our lottery tickets had a great effect; a great part of that prize will come to our pockets."

Said my friend Hassan smiling at the moment that he saw me walk through his door.

"That means that we won the lottery? I really don't believe it!" I answered, appearing somewhat unbelieving.

Asking me what I was going to do, or in what I was going to invest my part of the prize, he told me laughing:

"Believe it, man."

As he gave me part of the prize that corresponded to me.

"The first thing I will do is resign from my job, pay all my past due debts, buy a penthouse in Manhattan with a view of Central Park and take some long and well deserved vacation through the Mediterranean, Ipanema, Honolulu and Kuala Lumpur."

I answered laughing out loud, as I took the ten dollars that were my part of the prize.

"You know that I will do exactly the same with mine, but the difference is that mine will be in Oceania so that I can call you from the other side of the world."

Answered my friend Hassan, laughing out loud.

His store turned into a small circus every time I went to visit him. It was my obligatory dosage of laugher of each afternoon before I got home. Thinking about what I was going to spend my prize in, in addition to what I mentioned earlier, after saying goodbye to my friend Hassan, I continued on my way home, walking in the middle of that snow storm that was beginning to cover the city in white.

In spite that I had a lot of material to digitize in my computer, the three bed, and forced me to stop the story that I had been writing to recharge my energies through well deserved rest. My exhaustion was such, that I allowed the routine to overcome my will, so I prepared everything for the following day, just like I always did.

To be sure that the exhaustion would not beat me, I gave the honor of waking me up to my old clock on the wall. As if I it was a well behaved child, fulfilling the order that I had imposed the night before, at exactly six in the morning the first frequency of unpleasant sound to any eardrum, burst into the entire room waking me up from the trance I had fallen in. I programed it half an hour before usual, so that when I got up I could gain momentum with each sound interval.

Chapter 5

Friday, Unexpected News

It's Friday, great. Another start to the weekend, that means a break from the diet and it's payday, I told myself laughing as I stood up. When I looked out the window, I noticed that the snowstorm had stopped, but it had left a great accumulation as a memento that complicated street and sidewalk movement through the city. Worst yet, interfering with the punctual schedule of public transportation, which means leaving with several minutes of anticipation to take the metro. The routine, as a vendetta for my act of rebellion of the past days, that morning before leaving the house she had a not very pleasant surprise that left a bit sad.

Like every morning, and this wasn't going to be the exception, after getting ready and doing the things that I was accustomed to before leaving, along with my inevitable cup of tea, I sat down to watch the news on the television without imagining that, that morning it would have a different nuance for me. A new face suddenly appeared in the weather forecast, announcing that she was going to cover the vacation days of my platonic love. This made me canceled my trip to heaven, because surprisingly, the creator of my special mornings wasn't there. Now, without a reason to be in front of the television, I turned it off, promising myself that I would

That morning, I left my house towards the subway station without knowing that, that day my life would take a completely unexpected turn. As I was entering the station, I noticed something different that I was not used to see. Mysteriously, my friend was not anywhere that morning; I looked up and down the platform to see if I would catch him, but I was unable to see him anywhere; therefore, I returned to the same spot where I used to board the metro, giving him time to appear, but it was useless.

As I was walking I asked myself: *why didn't my friend appear today?* At that time I was expecting to find Mathew so he could give me the news, but curiously he didn't show up that morning either, which left me a bit worried. Before going into work, I was getting ready psychologically to *"pretend to have deaf ears"* in respect to the scolding I was going to receive from my boss; he would surely be waiting to lecture me, but it wasn't necessary. Surprisingly he had also taken the day off and the person in charge of my section covered my back and my punishment would only be to have a few figures off my check.

As the hour to get off was near, unexplainably, a very unusual and uncommon sensation in me began to alter my entire interior making me feel uneasy and nervous. Aside from that weird sensation that at times made me feel overwhelmed, thanks to my coworker that covered my back with my boss, I was able to finish my work day calmly and without delay. Satisfied for having fulfilled with another week of work, I was on my way back home.

"But what face do you have today, I see that you didn't have a good day…that mood is not of a person that won the lottery. Cheer up, it's Friday!"

My friend Hassan said with a big smile as I went into his store to chat for a moment with him.

"In effect, today was a wonderful day, but inexplicably hours before leaving work, I began to feel an unusual and out of the ordinary sensation in me, which at times caused me sadness, melancholy and even anxiety. That's probably why I have this face."

I answered, pretending to smile.

"Relax man, that happens to all of us. Many times it's due to the sudden changes in mood, but there's nothing a multi vitamin shake, with secret homemade formulas to improve the mood of anyone."

Hassan said, as he began to make that shake that contained a great variety of fruits and some secrets patented by him.

Thanking him for his cheerful words, but especially for the miraculous shake, I left his store towards my house without imagining what was about to happen; better yet, of what I was going to find out that might which made me discover the origin of that strange sensation that inexplicably overcame me.

It was Friday, it meant a break from my diet and the usual; trying to simply such time and like I used to do every Friday, I replaced my culinary skills for something simple and fast from a restaurant. Adding a great quantity of hot chocolate to that night's purchased dinner, I went home planning in my head to continue writing the story that was pending. Of course, this would be after the cinematic premier that I was used to watch every last workday. As I was getting ready to go to the movies, after sharing a delicious dinner with roommates, I did something unusual that made me cancel at the last minute everything that I had planned for that night. In spite that I daily saw the newspaper in the dining room table that

Danny, one of my roommates, had brought home. The news that was inside, perhaps would not kill, but madden anyone that was in a situation similar to mine.

"AFTER REMAINING IN COMA FOR FOUR DAYS, A MAN WHO WAS RUN OVER BY THE TRAIN LAST MONDAY IN THE METRO STATION DIES", read the headline on top of the picture of the victim in one of the pages that gave me the curiosity to read. When I recognized the photo of my friend who was the principal protagonists of that headline, aside from the chills that ran through my body and that I almost lost consciousness, my mind took a sudden step back in time, going back to the first day I met him; trying to decipher a few things that he said that day and that I didn't understand. Amongst the things that I discovered was first the watch that had been robbed from him and this happened because the train tore off the arm that he wore it on. In respect to waiting for orders from his superiors to go to another place, I understood that the entire time he was talking about the supreme power of the universe to

and ruthlessly threw him towards the train tracks at the precise moment that it was arriving at the station; they didn't leave enough time for any maneuver to escape the mortal weight of all that tonnage of steel.

Without saying a word to my roommates; after having read that article, guided solely by my intuition and locked in a frightening atmosphere that invaded my entire body, I headed towards my room to think, denying the belief of what was happening. The people that were looking at me in the train with awe were right, *"the crazy one there was me"*, I said to myself, trying to understand why those things were happening to me. Also, I was slamming my fist into the wall so that the pain would make me forget what happened. At times I wanted to tell my roommates, but it would have been useless, because they would not have believed it. Feeling alone, and having no one to tell what was happening, I locked myself in my room to wait for the next day and look for Mathew; he would help understand the situation, because I was gradually losing my mind.

Leaving the light on, my computer and any electrical devise in my room so that it would help me stay awake, I began to walk in circles; walking from one spot to another overwhelmed by the fear that I began to feel at that instant. After walking for several hours in my room, without receiving any sign of dawn, I sat confused and disoriented in a corner as I painted the floor red as a result of my hand's hemorrhage caused by slamming it against the wall. From that moment I remember absolutely nothing until the following day when I felt the discomfort and cold of the floor that woke me up after having slept for several hours; at that moment it was ten in morning of a new day: Saturday.

Chapter 6

Saturday, Looking for Answers

At that moment all I wanted was to clear my doubts and know what was going on. Guided by my intuition more than my senses I left towards the metro to hunt down Mathew. He was the only one that could help me. When I didn't see him board the train from any of the station I thought I would find him in, I headed towards that viewpoint that two days earlier they had taken me to; as I was getting closer I could hear several people that were practicing the anti stress therapy that my two friends showed me. The closer I got made my confidence that I would find him grow, but it was useless, tired of waiting a long time without any traces of them, I headed towards the other side of the island where we had our breakfast (*under the Brooklyn Bridge*). I was hoping to find their friends so that they could give me the coordinates of their whereabouts, but when I arrived I found another surprise. That place had been closed for a long time due to reconstruction of the structure; I only found several men doing construction work. It was then that I began to feel more worried because I felt as if logic was abandoning me, giving madness the advantage in respect to my sanity, because I was witness to the emptiness of that place and that Mathew's friends found refuge in that spot.

resident of the seventh floor of that building. As I was on the metro on my way to that foundation, my mind was threatening to abandon me, and began to remind me of each strange thing that my friend either said or did; not allowing me to believe that Mathew was also an spectrum that I had been talking to for nearly a week.

When I arrived at the foundation, almost in front of the entrance, I saw our snow doubles that were posing next to the bus stop; they were completely intact and even wearing the piece of clothing that each one of us had placed as part of a better presentation. I took a breath of relief telling myself *"ghosts cannot do things like these"*, while I began to doubt that my friend was the protagonist of the news that I read in the paper the night before, which made formulate doubts, testing my entire mental state. Surely it must be someone very similar to my friend and I am imagining other things, I told myself as I crossed the door towards the inside of the foundation.

"I see that you are once again visiting us. This time, I would be your guide."

She said smiling, the same person on the reception that received me two days earlier.

"This time to my visit is not tour your facilities, but in effect the next time I return you will be my guide. The reason for my presence here is to look for a friend that used to come to this place to spend the night and have something to eat."

I answered, making an effort to smile

"We have a registry of all the people that enter this place. If you give me the name of the person you're looking for, then I will gladly help you."

The receptionist kindly answered.

"The only thing I know is that his name is Mathew and he is homeless." I said as he kept on looking in the computer.

"I'm sorry, but the registry does not show any person with that name. The only Mathew I know is he."

She answered as she pointed at a large painting with Mathew's face hung in the walls of the entrance of the foundation.

In the last visit I had not seen it, but it was effectively Mathew's picture. "Yes, he's the person I am looking for."

I answered astounded.

"I can't believe that you know Mr. Mathew; he was the founder and the one that built this place. Everyone that knew him said that he was an exceptional person."

The woman answered, somewhat surprised to my affirmation.

"*He was? ...You said that Mathew was?* You mean that Mathew is, because he still exists."

I answered a bit confused.

"It's impossible that you know Mister Mathew. He died several years ago."

She answered with some severity as if I was making fun of her.

"It's impossible. It was he who brought me to see this place two days ago, and it was he who showed me step by step the facilities of this place."

I answered completely confused and nervous.

"*Ah!* I see what you were referring to when you said that you had your own guide last time. You seem a bit tired; you should go rest and sleep a little. That's perhaps why you're seeing things that don't exist."

The receptionist answered with a tired smile as she began to narrate part of Mathew's life as she was trying to calm me down.

"Mr. Mathew was extremely wealthy and powerful owner of several firms that generated millions in profits. He was a man that was dedicated one hundred percent to his work in spite that he loved with his would his wife and son, his only family; he dedicated more time to his businesses than spending more time with them. At that time, he was prosperous and helped many people. But as he was giving his entire life to making money, he forgot about his family until a terrible hereditary mortal and silent illness overtook his wife and son. He was not with them to enjoy in life, not even help them during their ailment with the disease; he only noticed when it was too late and they passed away. This made him feel guilty and miserable for not having had dedicated more time to his family, then he decided to give up of all his fortunes and gave it all to charity. It was he who made this place possible, which by the way bears his name. Aside from that, he left enough funds for the maintenance of this place for several more years. It is said that after that, he began to wander through the drove him to worry more about making money to keep on aiding social causes, even by sacrificing the well being of his own family. He was a man worthy of admiration and always will be remembered by all of us and by everyone that knew him."

The receptionist finished with that.

"I don't know if it was my imagination or my mind playing tricks on me, but I'm sure that I met Mathew and he is exactly as you just described it to me."

I said smiling while I said goodbye to her.

All the fear, anxiety, and desperation that I felt, after leaving that place surprisingly disappeared. A sensation of peace and tranquility suddenly began to take over my entire body, which helped to take the metro back home. If Mathew and my friend appeared to me is because the universe wanted it that way; moreover, it was a good experience from which I learned several valuable things and I see no reason why I should feel fear or be scared. On the contrary, I should be thankful with life for having taken me into account to continue learning, I told myself as metro was taking me back home.

Worried because I didn't arrive to our date in the usual place, my girlfriend had decided to go and look for me at my house to make sure that I was fine. In spite that I had formulated an idea of what had happened, at times I couldn't stop feeling confused and disoriented. But thanks to a tight hug that my beautiful girlfriend gave me when I got home, peace and tranquility, which had abandoned me, returned to my body. When I saw her there, along with my roommates, who were also worriedly waiting for me, I came down. Since I had a knot on my throat, and my head a bit stunned, I felt as if I couldn't deal with all that had happened to me alone, so I looked at them and in a tearful hug I let go of all the pain that I felt at that moment. I thanked them for their worries and told them that everything was fine; I took my girlfriend by her hand and walked to my room to tell her what had happened.

While she nursed the wound on my hand that I stupidly gave myself while I smashed it against the wall, I laid on her lap and began to tell her every detail of what happened with Mathew and my friend; from the first day I met them, to the moment when I was talking to her.

If the universe gave us its best creation, it was not only for pleasure or to keep us company, but so it could be our complement, our support, our medicine for loneliness and especially so it could be our reason to be happy. It took only a few words from my beautiful girlfriend to make me feel completely relieved; making me notice that in contrast to what it appeared, what happened was something special. It was a gift from the universe so that it could extend my sight towards the sensibility of life, since there are things that are not simply seen by the eyes on our face.

Accompanied by her for the rest of the weekend, extremely content and happy, as if it was the last day of my life, we began to visit several places and friend that we hadn't seen in some time. As if it was the last time that we were going to see them, we called our families to tell them that we loved and missed them a lot; displaying affection that was more sincere than usual.

Sunday afternoon, I took her to the places that I went with Mathew and my friend to show her the practice of anti stress therapy that gave good results. Later, I took her where I had the most special breakfast of my life in company of wonderful people. When the afternoon was over, I took her to visit Mathew's foundation so that she would know his work. She was very active social service works and she thought it was a very special place. So much so, that she was making plans to rend her voluntary services to that foundation. Lastly, and before we took the metro to accompany her and leave her safe in her house, I took her to see our snowmen doubles that were still there thanks to the low temperature that was going to least a good while to evaporate. When she recognized the hat that my snowman wore, which also was part of her gift on my last birthday, she softly hugged and caressed it. She joked with me to not get jealous and gave it a kiss; she did the same with my other frosty friends.

After having shared unforgettable moments with my girlfriend, when we were at the door of her, she gave me a hug filled with love and a special and magical goodbye kiss. A kiss and hug that were tattooed in my soul for the rest of my life.

When I arrived at my house, I caught up with all my things and got

Epilogue

Monday, An Encounter with Destiny

$\mathcal{A}$ cold December morning in the Babel of Iron, my mind programmed for the routine, or actually a prisoner to it, activating the tick tock of punctuality attached to subconscious, which ordered me to get up. I was starting a new week and there were obligations to fulfill. After what happened, everything demonstrated that it would be an ordinary day like the rest in my life, but something else was about to happen.

Like always, I came out of my house to take the metro so that it would take me work, but before leaving the house, I took the newspaper cutout that showed that tragic news of my friend, I put it next to my computer and I premeditatedly left it on with the open file that contained the story that I was writing, which only needed one detail to reach its end.

Once inside the station, at the moment that the train was arriving, I walked towards the edge of the platform like I always did, suddenly I felt a strong push on my back that took me to the train tracks with no time to react. My brain acted as a defense mechanism, and it turned off completely at that instant. Even though I felt the entire weight of that machine crushing my bones, I came out floating without a single scratch and, incredibly, in less than a second I appeared at the next station where that there was nothing more to teach me, and then they were lost in the crowd and left me only with a goodbye hug.

With the excuse of asking the time, I went up to talk to a man that appeared to be very sad and worried. I ended up talking to him for a long while. After accompanying him to his work and going around the city several times, I came back home in the afternoon. At that time, Danny, one of my roommates, read the headline from the cut out that I left next to my computer along with the story in it, preparing him so that he would then write his own history.

Before leaving the house, I had previously left a written note on the dining room table, allowing him to go into my room so that he could do what the note asked.

Using the power that is provided by being an universal citizen, through him, and using his hands, I was able to finish this story. Once he finished writing, I made sure that he saved the file and then turn off my computer, and then let him cry for my departure....

- The End -